Short Stories of the Nineteenth Century

BLACKIE & SON LIMITED
16/18 William IV Street, Charing Cross, LONDON, W.C.2
17 Stanhope Street, GLASGOW

BLACKIE & SON (INDIA) LIMITED
103/5 Fort Street, BOMBAY

BLACKIE & SON (CANADA) LIMITED
TORONTO

Short Stories
of the
Nineteenth Century

SELECTED WITH INTRODUCTION

BY

J. G. FYFE, M.A.

BLACKIE & SON LIMITED
LONDON AND GLASGOW

Blackie's Standard English Classics

With Introduction and Notes

A Selection

AUSTEN—**Northanger Abbey.** R. F. Patterson, M.A., D.Litt.

BEAUMONT and FLETCHER—**The Knight of the Burning Pestle.** R. F. Patterson, M.A., D.Litt.

BROWNING—**Strafford.** Agnes Wilson.

CHAUCER—**Chaucer's Canterbury Pilgrims.** William Ferguson, M.A.
The Nonne Prest his Tale. R. F. Patterson, M.A., D.Litt.
The Prologue to the Canterbury Tales. R. F. Patterson, M.A., D.Litt.

DRYDEN—**Essay of Dramatic Poesy.** D. Nichol Smith, M.A.

English Essays. A Representative Anthology. W. Cuthbert Robb, M.A.

GOLDSMITH—**The Citizen of the World.** Selected Letters. W. A. Brockington, M.A.
She Stoops to Conquer. H. Littledale, M.A., Litt.D.
The Good-natured Man. H. Littledale, M.A., Litt.D.

KEATS—**Select Poems.** Isabella, Hyperion, The Eve of St. Agnes, and Lamia. J. H. Boardman, B.A.(Lond.), L.C.P.

KINGLAKE—**Eothen.** Including the Author's own notes. Introduction by Sir Arthur T. Quiller-Couch.

LAMB—**Select Tales from Shakespeare.** David Frew, B.A.

LONGFELLOW—**The Song of Hiawatha.**

MACAULAY — **England in 1685.** (The Third Chapter of "Macaulay's History".) H. Clement Notcutt, B.A., Ph.D.
Lives of Johnson and Goldsmith. John Downie, M.A.

MARLOWE—**Dr. Faustus.** R. G. Lunt, M.A.(Oxon.).
Edward the Second. R. G. Lunt, M.A.(Oxon.).

MILTON—**Lycidas.** H. B. Cotterill.
Paradise Lost. Books I, II, III. F. Gorse, M.A. (In separate vols.)
Paradise Lost. Books V and VI. A. Roberts, M.A. (In separate vols.)
Samson Agonistes. Sir Edmund K. Chambers, K.B.E., C.B., M.A., D.Litt.

POPE—**Rape of the Lock.** Frederick Ryland, M.A.

SCOTT—**The Lady of the Lake. The Lay of the Last Minstrel.**

SHERIDAN—**The Critic.** R. F. Patterson, M.A., D.Litt.

SPENSER—**The Faery Queene.** Book I. W. Keith Leask, M.A.
The Faery Queene. Book II. W. Keith Leask, M.A.
The Faery Queene. Book V. E. H. Blakeney, M.A.

TENNYSON — **The Coming of Arthur, The Passing of Arthur, and Gareth and Lynette.** David Frew, B.A., and R. F. Patterson, D.Litt.

BLACKIE & SON LIMITED, LONDON AND GLASGOW

Printed in Great Britain by Blackie & Son, Ltd., Glasgow

CONTENTS

INTRODUCTION

The love of a good story is almost as old as the human race itself. Before there was any literature, even before men could write, the telling of stories was the chief form of entertainment at family gatherings, and the best of such stories, handed down by oral tradition, have survived to this day in the great masses of folk-lore attached to almost every race in the world. Some of these stories have been collected and printed, others have still no settled form, and vary with every telling round the evening fire in the Hebridean islands, on the Asiatic steppes, or in the American Indian reserves.

Much of the earliest literature in the world, too, consists of stories. The literatures of Persia, Arabia, and China, of the Jews, the Greeks, and the Romans, abound in tales of gods and heroes and ordinary men, as witness the *Bible*, the *Arabian Nights*, the *Iliad*, the *Odyssey*, and the *Aeneid*.

The recognition, however, of the short story *as a distinct form of literary art* is comparatively recent. Prior to the nineteenth century short stories were frequently, though not always, little more than condensed novels weighed down by an army of characters and by a plethora of thinly connected incidents. In the nineteenth century, however, the short story came into its own, partly because the great increase in the number of magazines specializing in fiction provided authors with a market which had hitherto been lacking. Early in the century, Edgar Allan Poe, himself one of the masters of this literary form, wrote: "The increase, within a few years, of the magazine literature, is by no means to be regarded as indicating what some critics would suppose it to indicate—a downward tendency in taste or in letters. It is but a sign of the times, an indication of an era in which men are forced upon the curt, the condensed, the well-digested, in place of the voluminous." This dictum, wholly true when it was made, is now largely of historical interest. The "swiftness" of the present age, with its characteristic impatience, incapacity for sustained concentration, and interest in snippets and superficialities, may account for the ever-increasing demand for fiction magazines, but the majority of the stories printed in such magazines have no value as literary productions. They represent, if you like, the elemental short story, though the best of them may have something in common with the short story which Poe had in mind, but not with that which he himself actually wrote.

The true short story is an artistic masterpiece. What it requires of the author we shall see later; what it demands of the reader are a high degree of mental concentration and a fine critical faculty. It cannot be skimmed in a tramway-car or a railway compartment, or used as an entrée at luncheon.

This literary form imposes certain restrictions on the author, and considerations of space make it essential that he should keep constantly before him what he is attempting to do and the effect he is striving to produce. A certain class of critics goes further even than this, and asserts that the perfect short story must observe unity of time, unity of place, and unity of action, just as if it were a one-act play. We do not propose to discuss the question of unity here—the reader can, if he wishes, do that for himself after he has read the stories in the book. All that need be said is that few of the masters of the art of short story writing have troubled about unity of time, place, or action, and that their work is certainly not weaker on that account. The one unity that they all observe is unity of effect—and that is the only one that matters.

Restrictions of space, of course, make terseness essential, and in a short story there is, therefore, no room for redundancy, or irrelevancy, or a multitude of characters. As a general rule, the author has to avoid complexity, without becoming merely superficial. Indeed, the construction of some stories (Edgar Allan Poe's *Cask of Amontillado*, for example) is so simple that the reader cannot but marvel at the effect produced.

This need for the avoidance of complexity in construction naturally affects the whole development of a short story. The evolution of the plot, no matter how profound that plot may be, or of the author's aim, must come from within the story —all the parts of the puzzle must be laid before the reader and pieced together or disintegrated before his eyes. Read, for example, Washington Irving's *Rip Van Winkle* or Sir Walter Scott's *Wandering Willie's Tale*, and observe the perfect unity of effect, the natural development, and the apparent complete lack of effort.

But the ease with which a good story flows is deceptive, and it is in this that the author's art lies. The story-teller at the tribal gatherings talked to audiences who liked to hear the same old stories, told in the same old way and introducing familiar phrases. Thus he did not need to be a creative artist, or to worry about arrangement of details; he simply told his stories in chronological order, and depended for effect solely on his voice. Also, he could see his audiences, and could deal with any signs of discontent or displeasure the moment they appeared.

The position of the modern author is much more difficult —his public is not a small social gathering of which he is a member, but a huge multitude of individuals. He is further handicapped, too, by the fact that he does not appeal to his public direct, but through the medium of print. Also, before his work reaches that stage it has to surmount a barrier of editors or publishers. Thus old stories and ingenuous narration will not do, and the only modern survivals of the ancient story-tellers are the bores who are said to haunt club smoking-rooms. Everything the modern author turns out has to be new and striking both in matter and in form, and even where he uses a conventional basic plot he has to adopt an individual standpoint, develop a new situation, or find a new solution if he wishes to sell his story and reach the public.

As with matter, so with form; well-worn phrases, rigid logical or chronological sequence, superfluity of detail will kill the work of any modern author. He must capture the reader's attention in the very first sentence, and he must see that he writes nothing to diminish that interest.

The same applies to the ending. At one time almost every story ended with an anti-climax; either with the conventional " And so they lived happily ever after ", or with an unconvincing statement of the future career of each and every character. This was a trait of the early nineteenth century, and survived even amongst the late Victorians, many of whom had a sentimental craze for following their characters beyond the narrative proper into a future better unrecorded. Such a close is always bad art, though it suited a sentimental and leisured age, and even yet appeals to those readers of bad fiction in whom sentiment outweighs discrimination. But the good writer has to avoid anti-climax at all costs—his story may end on a note of surprise or it may leave the reader at the height of an emotional experience, but no matter how abrupt the ending may seem to be, it must leave the reader completely satisfied.

The modern writer then is striving to produce an effect, but he must adopt the manner of spontaneity. To do this he has to use originality in determining the disposition of details which will give character to the story. It would appear, then, that the excellence of a short story depends, not on the artificial observance of constructive conventions, but, as in every other sphere of literary endeavour, on the ability and originality of the author in using a difficult medium.

The stories in this book were all written in the nineteenth century, and they are all stories which have survived, and will survive, on their own merits. In its appeal a good story does not belong to any one period of time. Some of the stories here, such as *S.W. and by W. ¾ W.* and *The Squire's Story*, could have been written only in the nineteenth century, while others, such as *Wandering Willie's Tale* and *Rip Van Winkle*, are of the type of story produced by men of genius in every age—but all are related by the bond of common excellence.

Also, these eleven stories do not illustrate, and are not intended to illustrate, the history of the short story in the nineteenth century. There is, for example, no story in the collection typical of the tedious moral and sentimental tales of almost unbelievably bad quality, which were produced in such numbers in the early part of the century. Indeed, the temporal limitation in the title is of secondary importance— the stories are presented not as " of the nineteenth century ", but as good stories.

Wandering Willie's Tale

SIR WALTER SCOTT

Walter Scott was born in Edinburgh in 1771. He studied law and was admitted an advocate in 1792. *The Lay of the Last Minstrel*, published in 1805, was immediately popular, and his literary reputation was further enhanced by *Marmion* (1808) and *The Lady of the Lake* (1810). *Waverley*, the first of his romantic historical novels, was published anonymously in 1814 and achieved a great success. In 1826 the failure of Ballantyne's printing business, of which he was a partner, brought him to the verge of ruin, but with supreme courage he determined to earn with his pen enough money to pay his creditors in full. His efforts ruined his health, and he died in 1832. Scott did not write many short stories, finding, like Dickens, the limitations of the form too irksome, but in *Wandering Willie's Tale* in *Redgauntlet* he produced one of the greatest short stories in the English language.

Ye maun have heard of Sir Robert Redgauntlet of that Ilk, who lived in these parts before the dear years. The country will lang mind him; and our fathers used to draw breath thick if ever they heard him named. He was out wi' the Hielandmen in Montrose's time; and again he was in the hills wi' Glencairn in the saxteen hundred and fifty-twa; and sae when King Charles the Second came in, wha was in sic favour as the Laird of Redgauntlet? He was knighted at Lonon court, wi' the King's ain sword; and being a redhot prelatist, he came down here, rampauging like a lion, with commissions of lieutenancy, (and of lunacy, for what I ken,) to put down a' the Whigs and Covenanters in the country. Wild wark they made of it; for the Whigs were as dour[1] as the Cavaliers were fierce, and it was which should first tire the other. Redgauntlet was aye for the strong hand; and his name is kend as wide in the country as Claverhouse's or Tam Dalyell's[2]. Glen, nor dargle, nor mountain, nor cave, could hide the puir hill-folk when Redgauntlet was out with bugle and bloodhound after them, as if they had been sae mony deer. And troth when they fand them, they didna mak muckle mair ceremony than a Hielandman wi' a roebuck—It was just, " Will ye tak the test[3]?"—if not, " Make ready—present—fire!"—and there lay the recusant.

Far and wide was Sir Robert hated and feared. Men thought he had a direct compact with Satan—that he was proof against steel—and that bullets happed aff his buff-coat like hailstanes from a hearth—that he had a mear[4] that would turn a hare on the side of Carrifragawns[5]—and muckle to the same purpose, of whilk mair anon. The best blessing they wared on him was, " Deil scowp[6] wi' Redgauntlet!" He wasna a bad maister to his ain folk though, and was weel aneugh liked by his tenants; and as for the lackies and troopers that raid out wi' him to the persecutions, as the Whigs caa'd those killing times, they wad hae drunken themsells blind to his health at ony time.

Now you are to ken that my gudesire lived on Red-

---

[1] Obstinate.   [2] According to the story, Redgauntlet was a Royalist or Cavalier—he assisted the Royalist efforts of Montrose (1644–45) and Glencairn (1653), and from the Restoration in 1660 till the Revolution in 1688 he was engaged in suppressing the Covenanters.   By Tories Scott means Royalists, and by Whigs, Covenanters or Presbyterians.

[3] The Test was an oath to which, in the days of the Covenanting struggle, all were required to subscribe, under the penalty of death.   [4] Mare.

[5] A precipitous side of a mountain in Moffatdale.   [6] Run away with.

gauntlet's grund—they ca' the place Primrose-Knowe.
We had lived on the grund, and under the Redgauntlets,
since the riding days, and lang before. It was a pleasant
bit; and I think the air is callerer[1] and fresher there than
ony where else in the country. It's a' deserted now;
and I sat on the broken door-cheek three days since, and
was glad I couldna see[2] the plight the place was in; but
that's a' wide o' the mark. There dwelt my gudesire,
Steenie Steenson, a rambling, rattling chiel he had been
in his young days, and could play weel on the pipes;
he was famous at " Hoopers and Girders "—a' Cumber-
land couldna touch him at " Jockie Lattin "—and he
had the finest finger for the backlilt between Berwick
and Carlisle. The like o' Steenie wasna the sort that
they made Whigs o'. And so he became a Tory, as they
ca' it, which we now ca' Jacobites, just out of a kind of
needcessity, that he might belang to some side or other.
He had nae ill-will to the Whig bodies, and liked little
to see the blude rin, though, being obliged to follow Sir
Robert in hunting and hosting, watching and warding,
he saw muckle mischief, and maybe did some, that he
couldna avoid.

Now Steenie was a kind of favourite with his master,
and kend a' the folks about the Castle, and was often
sent for to play the pipes when they were at their merriment. Auld Dougal MacCallum, the butler, that had
followed Sir Robert through gude and ill, thick and thin,
pool and stream, was specially fond of the pipes, and aye
gae my gudesire his gude word wi' the Laird; for Dougal
could turn his master round his finger.

Weel, round came the Revolution, and it had like to
have broken the hearts baith of Dougal and his master.

<hr>

[1] Crisper.   [2] Wandering Willie was blind.

But the change was not a'thegether sae great as they feared, and other folk thought for. The Whigs made an unco crawing what they wad do with their auld enemies, and in special wi' Sir Robert Redgauntlet. But there were ower mony great folks dipped in the same doings, to mak a spick and span new warld. So Parliament passed it a' ower easy; and Sir Robert, bating that he was held to hunting foxes instead of Covenanters, remained just the man he was. His revel was as loud, and his hall as weel lighted, as ever it had been, though maybe he lacked the fines of the nonconformists,[1] that used to come to stock his larder and cellar; for it is certain he began to be keener about the rents than his tenants used to find him before, and they behoved to be prompt to the rent-day, or else the Laird wasna pleased. And he was sic an awsome body, that naebody cared to anger him; for the oaths he swore, and the rage that he used to get into, and the looks that he put on, made men sometimes think him a devil incarnate.

Weel, my gudesire was nae manager—no that he was a very great misguider—but he hadna the saving gift, and he got twa terms' rent in arrear. He got the first brash at Whitsunday put ower wi' fair word and piping; but when Martinmas came, there was a summons from the grund-officer to come wi' the rent on a day preceese, or else Steenie behoved to flit. Sair wark he had to get the siller; but he was weel-freended, and at last he got the haill scraped thegether—a thousand merks—the maist of it was from a neighbour they caa'd Laurie Lapraik—a sly tod[2]. Laurie had walth o' gear—could hunt wi' the hound and rin wi' the hare—and be Whig

---

[1] The fines exacted from Covenanters for non-attendance at church services conducted by Episcopalian clergymen. [2] Fox.

or Tory, saunt or sinner, as the wind stood. He was a professor in this Revolution warld, but he liked an orra sough [1] of this warld, and a tune on the pipes weel aneugh at a bytime, and abune a', he thought he had a gude security for the siller he lent my gudesire ower the stocking at Primrose-Knowe.

Away trots my gudesire to Redgauntlet Castle, wi' a heavy purse and a light heart, glad to be out of the Laird's danger. Weel, the first thing he learned at the Castle was, that Sir Robert had fretted himsell into a fit of the gout, because he did not appear before twelve o'clock. It wasna a'thegether for sake of the money, Dougal thought; but because he didna like to part wi' my gudesire aff the grund. Dougal was glad to see Steenie, and brought him into the great oak parlour, and there sat the Laird his leesome lane, excepting that he had beside him a great, ill-favoured jackanape [2], that was a special pet of his; a cankered beast it was, and mony an ill-natured trick it played—ill to please it was, and easily angered—ran about the haill castle—chattering and yowling, and pinching, and biting folk, especially before ill-weather, or disturbances in the state. Sir Robert caa'd it Major Weir, after the warlock that was burnt; [3] and few folk liked either the name or the conditions of the creature—they thought there was something in it by ordinar—and my gudesire was not just easy in his mind when the door shut on him, and he saw himself in the room wi' naebody but the Laird, Dougal MacCallum, and the Major, a thing that hadna chanced to him before.

Sir Robert sat, or, I should say, lay, in a great armed

[1] An occasional breath.   [2] Monkey.
[3] A celebrated wizard, executed at Edinburgh for sorcery and other crimes.

chair, wi' his grand velvet gown, and his feet on a cradle; for he had baith gout and gravel, and his face looked as gash and ghastly as Satan's. Major Weir sat opposite to him, in a red laced coat, and the Laird's wig on his head; and aye as Sir Robert girned wi' pain, the jackanape girned too, like a sheep's-head between a pair of tangs —an ill-faur'd, fearsome couple they were. The Laird's buff-coat was hung on a pin behind him, and his broad-sword and his pistols within reach; for he keepit up the auld fashion of having the weapons ready, and a horse saddled day and night, just as he used to do when he was able to loup on horseback, and away after ony of the hill-folk he could get speerings [1] of. Some said it was for fear of the Whigs taking vengeance, but I judge it was just his auld custom—he wasna gien to fear ony thing. The rental-book, wi' its black cover and brass clasps, was lying beside him; and a book of sculduddry [2] sangs was put betwixt the leaves, to keep it open at the place where it bore evidence against the Goodman of Primrose-Knowe, as behind the hand with his mails [3] and duties. Sir Robert gave my gudesire a look, as if he would have withered his heart in his bosom. Ye maun ken he had a way of bending his brows, that men saw the visible mark of a horse-shoe in his forehead, deep-dinted, as if it had been stamped there.

" Are ye come light-handed, ye son of a toom whistle?" said Sir Robert. " Zounds! if you are——"

My gudesire, with as gude a countenance as he could put on, made a leg, and placed the bag of money on the table wi' a dash, like a man that does something clever. The Laird drew it to him hastily—" Is it all here, Steenie, man?"

---

[1] Intelligence.　　　　[2] Obscene.　　　　[3] Rent.

" Your honour will find it right," said my gudesire.

" Here, Dougal," said the Laird, " gie Steenie a tass [1] of brandy down stairs, till I count the siller and write the receipt."

But they werena weel out of the room, when Sir Robert gied a yelloch that garr'd [2] the Castle rock. Back ran Dougal—in flew the livery-men—yell on yell gied the Laird, ilk ane mair awfu' than the ither. My gudesire knew not whether to stand or flee, but he ventured back into the parlour, where a' was gaun hirdy-girdie—naebody to say " come in ", or " gae out ". Terribly the Laird roared for cauld water to his feet, and wine to cool his throat; and hell, hell, hell, and its flames, was aye the word in his mouth. They brought him water, and when they plunged his swoln feet into the tub, he cried out it was burning; and folk say that it *did* bubble and sparkle like a seething caldron. He flung the cup at Dougal's head, and said he had given him blood instead of burgundy; and, sure aneugh, the lass washed clotted blood aff the carpet the neist day. The jackanape they caa'd Major Weir, it jibbered and cried as if it was mocking its master; my gudesire's head was like to turn —he forgot baith siller and receipt, and down stairs he banged; but as he ran, the shrieks came faint and fainter; there was a deep-drawn shivering groan, and word gaed through the Castle, that the Laird was dead.

Weel, away came my gudesire, wi' his finger in his mouth, and his best hope was, that Dougal had seen the money-bag, and heard the Laird speak of writing the receipt. The young Laird, now Sir John, came from Edinburgh, to see things put to rights. Sir John and his father never gree'd weel. Sir John had been bred

---

[1] Glass. [2] Made.

an advocate, and afterwards sat in the last Scots Parliament and voted for the Union, having gotten, it was
thought, a rug of the compensations [1]—if his father
could have come out of his grave, he would have brained
him for it on his awn hearthstane. Some thought it
was easier counting with the auld rough Knight than
the fair-spoken young ane—but mair of that anon.

Dougal MacCallum, poor body, neither grat nor
graned, but gaed about the house looking like a corpse,
but directing, as was his duty, a' the order of the grand
funeral. Now, Dougal looked aye waur and waur when
night was coming, and was aye the last to gang to his
bed, whilk was in a little round just opposite the chamber
of dais [2], whilk his master occupied while he was living,
and where he now lay in state, as they caa'd it, weel-
a-day! The night before the funeral, Dougal could keep
his awn counsel nae langer; he cam doun with his proud
spirit, and fairly asked auld Hutcheon to sit in his room
with him for an hour. When they were in the round,
Dougal took ae tass of brandy to himsell, and gave
another to Hutcheon, and wished him all health and
lang life, and said that, for himsell, he wasna lang for
this world; for that, every night since Sir Robert's death,
his silver call had sounded from the state-chamber,
just as it used to do at nights in his lifetime, to call
Dougal to help to turn him in his bed. Dougal said,
that being alone with the dead on that floor of the tower,
(for naebody cared to wake Sir Robert Redgauntlet like
another corpse,) he had never daured to answer the call,
but that now his conscience checked him for neglecting

---

[1] A reference to the popular belief that in 1707 many members of the
Scottish Parliament were bribed to vote in favour of the Act of Union.

[2] State bedroom.

his duty; for, " though death breaks service," said MacCallum, " it shall never break my service to Sir Robert; and I will answer his next whistle, so be you will stand by me, Hutcheon."

Hutcheon had nae will to the wark, but he had stood by Dougal in battle and broil, and he wad not fail him at this pinch; so down the carles sat ower a stoup of brandy, and Hutcheon, who was something of a clerk, would have read a chapter of the Bible; but Dougal would hear naething but a blaud [1] of Davie Lindsay, whilk was the waur preparation.

When midnight came, and the house was quiet as the grave, sure aneugh the silver whistle sounded as sharp and shrill as if Sir Robert was blowing it, and up gat the twa auld serving-men, and tottered into the room where the dead man lay. Hutcheon saw aneugh at the first glance; for there were torches in the room, which showed him the foul fiend, in his ain shape, sitting on the Laird's coffin! Over he cowped [2] as if he had been dead. He could not tell how lang he lay in a trance at the door, but when he gathered himself, he cried on his neighbour, and getting nae answer, raised the house, when Dougal was found lying dead within twa steps of the bed where his master's coffin was placed. As for the whistle, it was gaen anes and aye; but mony a time was it heard at the top of the house on the bartizan, and amang the auld chimneys and turrets, where the howlets have their nests. Sir John hushed the matter up, and the funeral passed over without mair bogle-wark [3].

But when a' was ower, and the Laird was beginning

---

[1] A fragment—here means a passage from the poetical works of Sir David Lindsay.   [2] Tumbled.   [3] Ghost-work.

to settle his affairs, every tenant was called up for his arrears, and my gudesire for the full sum that stood against him in the rental-book. Weel, away he trots to the Castle, to tell his story, and there he is introduced to Sir John, sitting in his father's chair, in deep mourning, with weepers and hanging cravat, and a small walking rapier by his side, instead of the auld broadsword, that had a hundred-weight of steel about it, what with blade, chape, and basket-hilt. I have heard their communing so often tauld over, that I almost think I was there mysell, though I couldna be born at the time.

"I wuss ye joy, sir, of the head seat, and the white loaf, and the braid lairdship. Your father was a kind man to friends and followers; muckle grace to you, Sir John, to fill his shoon—his boots, I suld say, for he seldom wore shoon, unless it were muils [1] when he had the gout."

"Ay, Steenie," quoth the Laird, sighing deeply and putting his napkin to his een, "his was a sudden call, and he will be missed in the country; no time to set his house in order—weel prepared Godward, no doubt, which is the root of the matter—but left us behind a tangled hesp [2] to wind, Steenie.—Hem! hem! We maun go to business, Steenie; much to do, and little time to do it in."

Here he opened the fatal volume. I have heard of a thing they call Doomsday-book—I am clear it has been a rental of back-ganging tenants.

"Stephen," said Sir John, still in the same soft, sleekit [3] tone of voice—"Stephen Stevenson, or Steenson, ye are down here for a year's rent behind the hand—due at last term."

---

[1] Slippers.   [2] Hank.   [3] Smooth.

Stephen. " Please your honour, Sir John, I paid it to your father."

Sir John. " Ye took a receipt then, doubtless, Stephen; and can produce it?"

Stephen. " Indeed I hadna time, an it like your honour; for nae sooner had I set doun the siller, and just as his honour Sir Robert, that's gaen, drew it till him to count it, and write out the receipt, he was ta'en wi' the pains that removed him."

" That was unlucky," said Sir John, after a pause. " But ye maybe paid it in the presence of somebody. I want but a *talis qualis* evidence, Stephen. I would go ower strictly to work with no poor man."

Stephen. " Troth, Sir John, there was naebody in the room but Dougal MacCallum the butler. But, as your honour kens, he has e'en followed his auld master."

" Very unlucky again, Stephen," said Sir John, without altering his voice a single note. " The man to whom ye paid the money is dead—and the man who witnessed the payment is dead too—and the siller, which should have been to the fore, is neither seen nor heard tell of in the repositories. How am I to believe a' this?"

Stephen. " I dinna ken, your honour; but there is a bit memorandum note of the very coins; for, God help me! I had to borrow out of twenty purses; and I am sure that ilka man there set down will take his grit oath for what purpose I borrowed the money."

Sir John. " I have little doubt ye *borrowed* the money, Steenie. It is the *payment* to my father that I want to have some proof of."

Stephen. " The siller maun be about the house, Sir John. And since your honour never got it, and his honour that was canna have ta'en it wi' him, maybe some of the family may have seen it."

Sir John. "We will examine the servants, Stephen; that is but reasonable."

But lackey and lass, and page and groom, all denied stoutly that they had ever seen such a bag of money as my gudesire described. What was waur, he had unluckily not mentioned to any living soul of them his purpose of paying his rent. Ae quean[1] had noticed something under his arm, but she took it for the pipes.

Sir John Redgauntlet ordered the servants out of the room, and then said to my gudesire, " Now, Steenie, ye see you have fair play; and, as I have little doubt ye ken better where to find the siller than ony other body, I beg, in fair terms, and for your own sake, that you will end this fasherie[2]; for, Stephen, ye maun pay or flit."

" The Lord forgie your opinion," said Stephen, driven almost to his wit's end—" I am an honest man."

" So am I, Stephen," said his honour; " and so are all the folks in the house, I hope. But if there be a knave amongst us, it must be he that tells the story he cannot prove." He paused, and then added, mair sternly, " If I understand your trick, sir, you want to take advantage of some malicious reports concerning things in this family, and particularly respecting my father's sudden death, thereby to cheat me out of the money, and perhaps take away my character, by insinuating that I have received the rent I am demanding.—Where do you suppose this money to be?—I insist upon knowing."

My gudesire saw every thing look sae muckle against him, that he grew nearly desperate—however, he shifted

---

[1] Girl.   [2] Trouble.

from one foot to another, looked to every corner of the room and made no answer.

"Speak out, sirrah," said the Laird, assuming a look of his father's, a very particular ane, which he had when he was angry—it seemed as if the wrinkles of his frown made that self-same fearful shape of a horse's shoe in the middle of his brow;—"Speak out, sir! I *will* know your thoughts;—do you suppose that I have this money?"

"Far be it frae me to say so," said Stephen.

"Do you charge any of my people with having taken it?"

"I wad be laith to charge them that may be innocent," said my gudesire; "and if there be any one that is guilty, I have nae proof."

"Somewhere the money must be, if there is a word of truth in your story," said Sir John; "I ask where you think it is—and demand a correct answer?"

"In hell, if you *will* have my thoughts of it," said my gudesire, driven to extremity,—"in hell! with your father, his jackanape, and his silver whistle."

Down the stairs he ran, (for the parlour was nae place for him after such a word,) and he heard the Laird swearing blood and wounds behind him, as fast as ever did Sir Robert, and roaring for the bailie and the baron-officer.

Away rode my gudesire to his chief creditor, (him they caa'd Laurie Lapraik,) to try if he could make onything out of him; but when he tauld his story, he got but the warst word in his wame [1]—thief, beggar, and dyvour [2], were the saftest terms; and to the boot of these hard terms, Laurie brought up the auld story of his dipping his hand in the blood of God's saunts [3], just as if a tenant

---

[1] Belly.   [2] An insolvent debtor.

[3] A reference to the persecution of the Covenanters (God's saints).

could have helped riding with the Laird, and that a laird
like Sir Robert Redgauntlet. My gudesire was, by this
time, far beyond the bounds of patience, and, while he
and Laurie were at deil speed the liars, he was wanchancie[1]
aneugh to abuse Lapraik's doctrine as weel as the man,
and said things that garr'd folk's flesh grue[2] that heard
them;—he wasna just himsell, and he had lived wi' a wild
set in his day.

At last they parted, and my gudesire was to ride hame
through the wood of Pitmurkie, that is a' fou of black
firs, as they say.—I ken the wood, but the firs may be
black or white for what I can tell.—At the entry of the
wood there is a wild common, and on the edge of the
common, a little lonely change-house[3], that was keepit
then by an ostler-wife, they suld hae caa'd her Tibbie
Faw, and there puir Steenie cried for a mutchkin of
brandy, for he had had no refreshment the haill day.
Tibbie was earnest wi' him to take a bite of meat, but
he couldna think o't, nor would he take his foot out of
the stirrup, and took off the brandy wholely at twa
draughts, and named a toast at each:—the first was, the
memory of Sir Robert Redgauntlet, and might he never
lie quiet in his grave till he had righted his poor bond-
tenant; and the second was, a health to Man's Enemy,
if he would but get him back the pock of siller, or tell
him what came o't, for he saw the haill world was like to
regard him as a thief and a cheat, and he took that waur
than even the ruin of his house and hauld.

On he rode, little caring where. It was a dark night
turned, and the trees made it yet darker, and he let the
beast take its ain road through the wood; when, all of
a sudden, from tired and wearied that it was before, the

---

[1] Unlucky.   [2] Shudder.   [3] Inn.

nag began to spring, and flee, and stend[1], that my gudesire could hardly keep the saddle—Upon the whilk, a
horseman, suddenly riding up beside him, said, " That's
a mettle beast of yours, freend; will you sell him?"—So
saying, he touched the horse's neck with his riding-
wand, and it fell into its auld heigh-ho of a stumbling
trot. " But his spunk's[2] soon out of him, I think,"
continued the stranger, " and that is like mony a man's
courage, that thinks he wad do great things till he come
to the proof."

My gudesire scarce listened to this, but spurred his
horse, with " Gude e'en to you, freend."

But it's like the stranger was ane that doesna lightly
yield his point; for, ride as Steenie liked, he was aye
beside him at the self-same pace. At last my gudesire,
Steenie Steenson, grew half angry; and, to say the truth,
half feared.

" What is it that ye want with me, freend?" he said.
" If ye be a robber, I have nae money; if ye be a leal
man, wanting company, I have nae heart to mirth or
speaking; and if ye want to ken the road, I scarce ken it
mysell."

" If you will tell me your grief," said the stranger, " I
am one that, though I have been sair miscaa'd in the
world, am the only hand for helping my freends."

So my gudesire, to ease his ain heart, mair than from
any hope of help, told him the story from beginning to
end.

" It's a hard pinch," said the stranger; " but I think
I can help you."

" If you could lend the money, sir, and take a lang
day[3]—I ken nae other help on earth," said my gudesire.

---

[1] Leap.   [2] Spirit.   [3] Be prepared to wait a long time for it.

"But there may be some under the earth," said the stranger. "Come, I'll be frank wi' you; I could lend you the money on bond, but you would maybe scruple my terms. Now, I can tell you, that your auld Laird is disturbed in his grave by your curses, and the wailing of your family, and if ye daur venture to go to see him, he will give you the receipt."

My gudesire's hair stood on end at this proposal, but he thought his companion might be some humorsome chield[1] that was trying to frighten him, and might end with lending him the money. Besides, he was bauld wi' brandy, and desperate wi' distress; and he said, he had courage to go to the gate of hell, and a step farther, for that receipt.—The stranger laughed.

Weel, they rode on through the thickest of the wood, when, all of a sudden, the horse stopped at the door of a great house; and, but that he knew the place was ten miles off, my father would have thought he was at Red-gauntlet Castle. They rode into the outer court-yard, through the muckle faulding yetts[2], and aneath the auld portcullis; and the whole front of the house was lighted, and there were pipes and fiddles, and as much dancing and deray[3] within as used to be in Sir Robert's house at Pace[4] and Yule, and such high seasons. They lap off, and my gudesire, as seemed to him, fastened his horse to the very ring he had tied him to that morning, when he gaed to wait on the young Sir John.

"God!" said my gudesire, "if Sir Robert's death be but a dream!"

He knocked at the ha' door just as he was wont, and his auld acquaintance, Dougal MacCallum,—just after his wont, too,—came to open the door, and said, "Piper

___
[1] Fellow.   [2] Folding gates.   [3] Disorder.   [4] Easter.

Steenie, are ye there, lad? Sir Robert has been crying for you."

My gudesire was like a man in a dream—he looked for the stranger, but he was gane for the time. At last he just tried to say, " Ha! Dougal Driveower, are ye living? I thought ye had been dead."

" Never fash yoursell wi' me," said Dougal, " but look to yoursell; and see ye tak naething frae onybody here, neither meat, drink, or siller, except just the receipt that is your ain."

So saying, he led the way out through halls and trances that were weel kend to my gudesire, and into the auld oak parlour; and there was as much singing of profane sangs, and birling of red wine, and speaking blasphemy and sculduddry, as had ever been in Redgauntlet Castle when it was at the blithest.

But, Lord take us in keeping! what a set of ghastly revellers they were that sat round that table!—My gudesire kend mony that had long before gane to their place, for often had he piped to the most part in the hall of Redgauntlet. There was the fierce Middleton, and the dissolute Rothes, and the crafty Lauderdale; and Dalyell, with his bald head and a beard to his girdle; and Earlshall, with Cameron's blude on his hand; and wild Bonshaw, that tied blessed Mr. Cargill's limbs till the blude sprang; and Dunbarton Douglas, the twice-turned traitor baith to country and king. There was the Bluidy Advocate MacKenyie, who, for his worldly wit and wisdom, had been to the rest as a god. And there was Claverhouse, as beautiful as when he lived, with his long, dark, curled locks streaming down over his laced buffcoat, and his left hand always on his right spuleblade, to hide the wound that the silver bullet had

made.[1] He sat apart from them all, and looked at them
with a melancholy, haughty countenance; while the rest
hallooed, and sung, and laughed, that the room rang.
But their smiles were fearfully contorted from time to
time; and their laughter passed into such wild sounds,
as made my gudesire's very nails grow blue, and chilled
the marrow in his banes.

They that waited at the table were just the wicked
serving-men and troopers, that had done their work and
cruel bidding on earth. There was the Lang Lad of the
Nethertown, that helped to take Argyle; and the Bishop's
summoner, that they called the Deil's Rattle-bag; and
the wicked guardsmen, in their laced coats; and the
savage Highland Amorites, that shed blood like water;
and many a proud serving-man, haughty of heart and
bloody of hand, cringing to the rich, and making them
wickeder than they would be; grinding the poor to
powder, when the rich had broken them to fragments.
And mony, mony mair were coming and ganging, a' as
busy in their vocation as if they had been alive.

Sir Robert Redgauntlet, in the midst of a' this fearful
riot, cried, wi' a voice like thunder, on Steenie Piper, to
come to the board-head where he was sitting; his legs
stretched out before him, and swathed up with flannel,
with his holster pistols aside him, while the great broad-
sword rested against his chair, just as my gudesire had
seen him the last time upon earth—the very cushion for
the jackanape was close to him, but the creature itsell
was not there—it wasna its hour, it's likely; for he heard
them say as he came forward, " Is not the Major come

<hr />

[1] All the persons mentioned were notorious persecutors of the Covenanters. The reference to Claverhouse's wound is based on the superstition
prevalent amongst the Covenanters that he could be killed only by a silver
bullet. The "spule-blade" is the shoulder-blade.

yet?" And another answered, " The jackanape will be
here betimes the morn." And when my gudesire came
forward, Sir Robert, or his ghaist, or the deevil in his
likeness, said, " Weel, piper, hae ye settled wi' my son
for the year's rent?"

With much ado my father gat breath to say, that Sir
John would not settle without his honour's receipt.

" Ye shall hae that for a tune of the pipes, Steenie,"
said the appearance of Sir Robert—" Play us up ' Weel
hoddled, Luckie '."

Now this was a tune my gudesire learned frae a warlock, that heard it when they were worshipping Satan
at their meetings; and my gudesire had sometimes
played it at the ranting suppers in Redgauntlet Castle,
but never very willingly; and now he grew cauld at the
very name of it, and said, for excuse, he hadna his pipes
wi' him.

" MacCallum, ye limb of Beelzebub," said the fearfu'
Sir Robert, " bring Steenie the pipes that I am keeping
for him!"

MacCallum brought a pair of pipes might have served
the piper of Donald of the Isles. But he gave my gudesire a nudge as he offered them; and looking secretly
and closely, Steenie saw that the chanter was of steel,
and heated to a white heat; so he had fair warning not
to trust his fingers with it. So he excused himself again,
and said, he was faint and frightened, and had not wind
aneugh to fill the bag.

" Then ye maun eat and drink, Steenie," said the
figure; " for we do little else here; and it's ill speaking
between a fou man and a fasting."

Now these were the very words that the bloody Earl
of Douglas said to keep the King's messenger in hand,

while he cut the head off MacLellan of Bombie, at the
Threave Castle; and that put Steenie mair and mair on
his guard. So he spoke up like a man, and said he came
neither to eat, or drink, or make minstrelsy; but simply
for his ain—to ken what was come o' the money he had
paid, and to get a discharge for it; and he was so stout-
hearted by this time, that he charged Sir Robert for
conscience-sake—(he had no power to say the holy name)
—and as he hoped for peace and rest, to spread no snares
for him, but just to give him his ain.

The appearance gnashed its teeth and laughed, but it
took from a large pocket-book the receipt, and handed
it to Steenie. " There is your receipt, ye pitiful cur;
and for the money, my dog-whelp of a son may go look
for it in the Cat's Cradle."

My gudesire uttered mony thanks, and was about to
retire, when Sir Robert roared aloud, " Stop though.
I am not done with thee. HERE we do nothing for nothing;
and you must return on this very day twelvemonth, to
pay your master the homage that you owe me for my
protection."

My father's tongue was loosed of a suddenty, and he
said aloud, " I refer mysell to God's pleasure, and not
to yours."

He had no sooner uttered the word than all was dark
around him; and he sunk on the earth with such a sudden
shock, that he lost both breath and sense.

How lang Steenie lay there, he could not tell; but
when he came to himsell, he was lying in the auld kirk-
yard of Redgauntlet parochine [1] just at the door of the
family aisle, and the scutcheon of the auld knight, Sir
Robert, hanging over his head. There was a deep morning

[1] Parish.

fog on grass and gravestane around him, and his horse
was feeding quietly beside the minister's twa cows.
Steenie would have thought the whole was a dream, but
he had the receipt in his hand, fairly written and signed
by the auld Laird; only the last letters of his name were
a little disorderly, written like one seized with sudden
pain.

Sorely troubled in his mind, he left that dreary place,
rode through the mist to Redgauntlet Castle, and with
much ado he got speech of the Laird.

"Well, you dyvour bankrupt," was the first word,
"have you brought me my rent?"

"No," answered my gudesire, "I have not; but I
have brought your honour Sir Robert's receipt for it."

"How, sirrah?—Sir Robert's receipt!—You told me he
had not given you one."

"Will your honour please to see if that bit line is
right?"

Sir John looked at every line, and at every letter, with
much attention; and at last, at the date, which my gudesire had not observed,—"*From my appointed place*," he
read, "*this twenty-fifth of November.*"—"What!—That is
yesterday!—Villain, thou must have gone to hell for
this!"

"I got it from your honour's father—whether he be
in heaven or hell, I know not," said Steenie.

"I will delate you for a warlock to the Privy Council,"
said Sir John. "I will send you to your master, the
devil, with the help of a tar-barrel and a torch.[1]"

"I intend to delate mysell to the Presbytery," said
Steenie, "and tell them all I have seen last night, whilk

---

[1] Sir John threatened to accuse (delate) Steenie before the Privy Council as
a wizard. He would then be burned at the stake. Steenie, on his part, said
that he would report his dealings with the devil to the all-powerful Presbytery.

are things fitter for them to judge of than a borrel ¹ man like me."

Sir John paused, composed himsell, and desired to hear the full history; and my gudesire told it him from point to point, as I have told it you—word for word, neither more nor less.

Sir John was silent again for a long time, and at last he said, very composedly, " Steenie, this story of yours concerns the honour of many a noble family besides mine; and if it be a leasing-making ², to keep yourself out of my danger, the least you can expect is to have a red-hot iron driven through your tongue, and that will be as bad as scauding your fingers with a red-hot chanter. But yet it may be true, Steenie; and if the money cast up, I shall not know what to think of it.—But where shall we find the Cat's Cradle? There are cats enough about the old house, but I think they kitten without the ceremony of bed or cradle."

" We were best ask Hutcheon," said my gudesire; " he kens a' the odd corners about as weel as—another serving-man that is now gane, and that I wad not like to name."

Aweel, Hutcheon, when he was asked, told them, that a ruinous turret, lang disused, next to the clock-house, only accessible by a ladder, for the opening was on the outside, and far above the battlements, was called of old the Cat's Cradle.

" There will I go immediately," said Sir John; and he took (with what purpose, Heaven kens) one of his father's pistols from the hall-table, where they had lain since the night he died, and hastened to the battlements.

It was a dangerous place to climb, for the ladder was

¹ Common.   ² Slander.

auld and frail, and wanted ane or twa rounds. However, up got Sir John, and entered at the turret door, where his body stopped the only little light that was in the bit turret. Something flees at him wi' a vengeance, maist dang[1] him back ower—bang gaed the knight's pistol, and Hutcheon, that held the ladder, and my gudesire that stood beside him, hears a loud skelloch[2]. A minute after, Sir John flings the body of the jackanape down to them, and cries that the siller is fund, and that they should come up and help him. And there was the bag of siller sure aneugh, and mony orra things besides, that had been missing for mony a day. And Sir John, when he had riped[3] the turret weel, led my gudesire into the dining-parlour, and took him by the hand, and spoke kindly to him, and said he was sorry he should have doubted his word, and that he would hereafter be a good master to him, to make amends.

"And now, Steenie," said Sir John, "although this vision of yours tends, on the whole, to my father's credit, as an honest man, that he should, even after his death, desire to see justice done to a poor man like you, yet you are sensible that ill-dispositioned men might make bad constructions upon it, concerning his soul's health. So, I think, we had better lay the haill dirdum[4] on that ill-deedie creature, Major Weir, and say naething about your dream in the wood of Pitmurkie. You had taken ower muckle brandy to be very certain about onything; and, Steenie, this receipt," (his hand shook while he held it out,)—"it's but a queer kind of document, and we will do best, I think, to put it quietly in the fire."

"Od, but for as queer as it is, it's a' the voucher I have for my rent," said my gudesire, who was afraid, it

---

[1] Knocked over.   [2] Screech.   [3] Searched.   [4] Mischief.

may be, of losing the benefit of Sir Robert's discharge.

"I will bear the contents to your credit in the rental-book, and give you a discharge under my own hand," said Sir John, "and that on the spot. And, Steenie, if you can hold your tongue about this matter, you shall sit, from this term downward, at an easier rent."

"Mony thanks to your honour," said Steenie, who saw easily in what corner the wind was; "doubtless I will be comfortable to all your honour's commands; only I would willingly speak wi' some powerful minister on the subject, for I do not like the sort of soumons of appointment whilk your honour's father——"

"Do not call the phantom my father!" said Sir John, interrupting him.

"Weel, then, the thing that was so like him," said my gudesire; "he spoke of my coming back to him this time twelvemonth, and it's a weight on my conscience."

"Aweel, then," said Sir John, "if you be so much distressed in mind, you may speak to our minister of the parish; he is a douce [1] man, regards the honour of our family, and the mair that he may look for some patronage from me."

Wi' that, my gudesire readily agreed that the receipt should be burnt, and the Laird threw it into the chimney with his ain hand. Burn it would not for them, though; but away it flew up the lum, wi' a lang train of sparks at its tail, and a hissing noise like a squib.

My gudesire gaed down to the manse, and the minister, when he had heard the story, said, it was his real opinion, that though my gudesire had gaen very far in tampering with dangerous matters, yet, as he had refused the devil's arles [2], (for such was the offer of meat and drink,) and had

---

[1] Sensible. [2] Earnest-money.

refused to do homage by piping at his bidding, he hoped,
that if he held a circumspect walk hereafter, Satan could
take little advantage by what was come and gane. And,
indeed, my gudesire, of his ain accord, long forswore
baith the pipes and the brandy—it was not even till the
year was out, and the fatal day passed, that he would
so much as take the fiddle, or drink usquebaugh or
tippenny.

Sir John made up his story about the jackanape as he
liked himsell; and some believe till this day there was
no more in the matter than the filching nature of the
brute. Indeed, ye'll no hinder some to threap [1], that it
was nane o' the Auld Enemy that Dougal and my gudesire saw in the Laird's room, but only that wanchancy
creature, the Major, capering on the coffin; and that,
as to the blawing on the Laird's whistle that was heard
after he was dead, the filthy brute could do that as weel
as the Laird himsell, if no better. But Heaven kens the
truth, whilk first came out by the minister's wife, after
Sir John and her ain gudeman were baith in the moulds.
And then my gudesire, wha was failed in his limbs, but
not in his judgment or memory—at least nothing to speak
of—was obliged to tell the real narrative to his freends,
for the credit of his good name. He might else have
been charged for a warlock.

[1] Maintain.

Rip Van Winkle

A POSTHUMOUS WRITING OF DIEDRICH KNICKERBOCKER [1]

WASHINGTON IRVING

Washington Irving was born of British parents at New York in 1783. He became a barrister, but his sole interest was literature, and in 1809 he published, using the psuedonym of Diedrich Knickerbocker, a burlesque entitled *A History of New York from the Beginning of the World to the End of the Dutch Dynasty*. In 1815 he came to Europe and spent the next seventeen years mainly in England and Spain. In this period he produced *The Sketch Book* (which contains his immortal story *Rip Van Winkle*), *Bracebridge Hall*, *Tales of a Traveller*, and *The Life of Columbus*. He returned to America in 1832, and from 1842 till 1846 was United States minister in Spain. He died in America in 1859. Irving, who excelled as an essayist, historian, and biographer, was the first great figure in American literary annals. His characteristics, however, were not American, but belonged rather to the age of Addison and Goldsmith.

> By Woden, God of Saxons,
> From whence comes Wensday, that is Wodensday.
> Truth is a thing that ever I will keep
> Unto thylke day in which I creep into
> My sepulchre————   CARTWRIGHT.

Whoever has made a voyage up the Hudson [2] must remember the Kaatskill mountains. They are a dis-

[1] "An old gentleman of New York, who was very curious in the Dutch history of the province, and the manners of the descendants from its primitive settlers."

[2] The river on which New York stands.

membered branch of the great Appalachian family, and
are seen away to the west of the river, swelling up to a
noble height, and lording it over the surrounding country.
Every change of season, every change of weather, indeed,
every hour of the day, produces some change in the
magical hues and shapes of these mountains, and they
are regarded by all the good wives, far and near, as perfect
barometers. When the weather is fair and settled, they
are clothed in blue and purple, and print their bold
outlines on the clear evening sky; but sometimes, when
the rest of the landscape is cloudless, they will gather a
hood of grey vapours about their summits, which, in
the last rays of the setting sun, will glow and light up
like a crown of glory.

At the foot of these fairy mountains, the voyager may
have descried the light smoke curling up from a village,
whose shingle-roofs gleam among the trees, just where
the blue tints of the upland melt away into the fresh
green of the nearer landscape. It is a little village, of
great antiquity, having been founded by some of the
Dutch colonists, in the early times of the province, just
about the beginning of the government of the good
Peter Stuyvesant [1] (may he rest in peace!), and there were
some of the houses of the original settlers standing within
a few years, built of small yellow bricks brought from
Holland, having latticed windows and gable fronts,
surmounted with weathercocks.

In that same village and in one of these very houses
(which, to tell the precise truth, was sadly time-worn and
weather-beaten), there lived many years since, while the
country was yet a province of Great Britain, a simple

[1] Dutch governor of New Amsterdam (now New York) from 1647 to
1665.

good-natured fellow, of the name of Rip Van Winkle. He was a descendant of the Van Winkles who figured so gallantly in the chivalrous days of Peter Stuyvesant, and accompanied him to the siege of Fort Christina. He inherited, however, but little of the martial character of his ancestors. I have observed that he was a simple good-natured man; he was, moreover, a kind neighbour, and an obedient henpecked husband. Indeed, to the latter circumstance might be owing that meekness of spirit which gained him such universal popularity, for those men are most apt to be obsequious and conciliating abroad, who are under the discipline of shrews at home. Their tempers, doubtless, are rendered pliant and malleable in the fiery furnace of domestic tribulation, and a curtain lecture is worth all the sermons in the world for teaching the virtues of patience and long-suffering. A termagant wife may, therefore, in some respects, be considered a tolerable blessing; and if so, Rip Van Winkle was thrice blessed.

Certain it is that he was a great favourite among all the good wives of the village, who, as usual with the amiable sex, took his part in all family squabbles, and never failed, whenever they talked those matters over in their evening gossipings, to lay all the blame on Dame Van Winkle. The children of the village, too, would shout with joy whenever he approached. He assisted at their sports, made their playthings, taught them to fly kites and shoot marbles, and told them long stories of ghosts, witches, and Indians. Whenever he went dodging about the village, he was surrounded by a troop of them, hanging on his skirts, clambering on his back, and playing a thousand tricks on him with impunity, and not a dog would bark at him throughout the neighbourhood.

The great error in Rip's composition was an insuperable
aversion to all kinds of profitable labour. It could not be
from the want of assiduity or perseverance, for he would
sit on a wet rock, with a rod as long and heavy as a Tartar's
lance, and fish all day without a murmur, even though he
should not be encouraged by a single nibble. He would
carry a fowling-piece on his shoulder for hours together,
trudging through woods and swamps, and up hill and
down dale, to shoot a few squirrels or wild pigeons. He
would never refuse to assist a neighbour even in the
roughest toil, and was a foremost man at all country
frolics for husking Indian corn, or building stone fences;
the women of the village, too, used to employ him to
run their errands, and to do such little odd jobs as their
less obliging husbands would not do for them. In a word,
Rip was ready to attend to anybody's business but his
own; but as to doing family duty, and keeping his farm
in order, he found it impossible.

In fact, he declared it was of no use to work on his
farm; it was the most pestilent little piece of ground in
the whole country; everything about it went wrong, and
would go wrong, in spite of him. His fences were continually falling to pieces; his cow would either go astray,
or get among the cabbages; weeds were sure to grow
quicker in his fields than anywhere else; the rain always
made a point of setting in just as he had some outdoor
work to do; so that though his patrimonial estate had
dwindled away under his management, acre by acre,
until there was little more left than a mere patch of
Indian corn and potatoes, yet it was the worst conditioned
farm in the neighbourhood.

His children, too, were as ragged and wild as if they
belonged to nobody. His son Rip, an urchin begotten

in his own likeness, promised to inherit the habits, with the old clothes of his father. He was generally seen trooping like a colt at his mother's heels, equipped in a pair of his father's cast-off galligaskins [1], which he had much ado to hold up with one hand, as a fine lady does her train in bad weather.

Rip Van Winkle, however, was one of those happy mortals, of foolish, well-oiled dispositions, who take the world easy, eat white bread or brown, whichever can be got with least thought or trouble, and would rather starve on a penny than work for a pound. If left to himself, he would have whistled life away in perfect contentment; but his wife kept continually dinning in his ears about his idleness, his carelessness, and the ruin he was bringing on his family. Morning, noon, and night, her tongue was incessantly going, and everthing he said or did was sure to produce a torrent of household eloquence. Rip had but one way of replying to all lectures of the kind, and that, by frequent use, had grown into a habit. He shrugged his shoulders, shook his head, cast up his eyes, but said nothing. This, however, always provoked a fresh volley from his wife; so that he was fain to draw off his forces, and take to the outside of the house—the only side, which, in truth, belongs to a hen-pecked husband.

Rip's sole domestic adherent was his dog Wolf, who was as much hen-pecked as his master; for Dame Van Winkle regarded them as companions in idleness, and even looked upon Wolf with an evil eye, as the cause of his master's going so often astray. True it is, in all points of spirit befitting an honourable dog, he was as courageous an animal as ever scoured the woods—but what courage

---

[1] Wide breeches.

can withstand the ever-during and all-besetting terrors of a woman's tongue? The moment Wolf entered the house, his crest fell, his tail drooped to the ground, or curled between his legs, he sneaked about with a gallows air, casting many a side-long glance at Dame Van Winkle, and at the least flourish of a broomstick or ladle, he would fly to the door with yelping precipitation.

Times grew worse and worse with Rip Van Winkle as years of matrimony rolled on; a tart temper never mellows with age, and a sharp tongue is the only edged tool that grows keener with constant use. For a long while he used to console himself, when driven from home, by frequenting a kind of perpetual club of the sages, philosophers, and other idle personages of the village, which held its sessions on a bench before a small inn, designated by a rubicund portrait of his Majesty George the Third. Here they used to sit in the shade through a long lazy summer's day, talking listlessly over village gossip, or telling endless sleepy stories about nothing. But it would have been worth any statesman's money to have heard the profound discussions that sometimes took place, when by chance an old newspaper fell into their hands from some passing traveller. How solemnly they would listen to the contents, as drawled out by Derrick Van Bummel, the schoolmaster, a dapper learned little man, who was not to be daunted by the most gigantic word in the dictionary; and how sagely they would deliberate upon public events some months after they had taken place.

The opinions of this junto were completely controlled by Nicholas Vedder, a patriarch of the village, and landlord of the inn, at the door of which he took his seat from morning till night, just moving sufficiently to avoid the sun and keep in the shade of a large tree, so that the neighbours could tell the hour by his movements as accurately as by a sundial. It is true he was rarely heard to speak, but smoked his pipe incessantly. His adherents, however (for every great man has his adherents), perfectly understood him, and knew how to gather his opinions. When anything that was read or related displeased him, he was observed to smoke his pipe vehemently, and to send forth short, frequent, and angry puffs; but when pleased he would inhale the smoke slowly and tranquilly, and emit it in light and placid clouds; and sometimes, taking the pipe from his mouth, and letting the fragrant vapour curl about his nose, would gravely nod his head in token of perfect approbation.

From even this stronghold the unlucky Rip was at length routed by his termagant wife, who would suddenly break in upon the tranquillity of the assemblage and call the members all to naught; nor was that august personage, Nicholas Vedder himself, sacred from the daring tongue of this terrible virago, who charged him outright with encouraging her husband in habits of idleness.

Poor Rip was at last reduced almost to despair; and his only alternative, to escape from the labour of the farm and clamour of his wife, was to take gun in hand and stroll away into the woods. Here he would some-times seat himself at the foot of a tree, and share the contents of his wallet with Wolf, with whom he sympathized as a fellow-sufferer in persecution. " Poor Wolf," he would say, " thy mistress leads thee a dog's life of it; but never mind, my lad, whilst I live thou shalt never want a friend to stand by thee!" Wolf would wag his tail, look wistfully in his master's face, and if dogs can feel pity, I verily believe he reciprocated the senti-ment with all his heart.

In a long ramble of the kind on a fine autumnal day, Rip had unconsciously scrambled to one of the highest parts of the Kaatskill mountains. He was after his favourite sport of squirrel-shooting, and the still solitudes had echoed and re-echoed with the reports of his gun. Panting and fatigued, he threw himself, late in the afternoon, on a green knoll, covered with mountain herbage, that crowned the brow of a precipice. From an opening between the trees he could overlook all the lower country for many a mile of rich woodland. He saw at a distance the lordly Hudson, far, far below him, moving on its silent but majestic course, with the reflection of a purple cloud, or the sail of a lagging bark, here and there sleeping on its glassy bosom, and at last losing itself in the blue highlands.

On the other side he looked down into a deep mountain glen, wild, lonely, and shagged, the bottom filled with fragments from the impending cliffs, and scarcely lighted by the reflected rays of the setting sun. For some time Rip lay musing on this scene; evening was gradually advancing; the mountains began to throw their long blue shadows over the valleys; he saw that it would be dark long before he could reach the village, and he heaved a heavy sigh when he thought of encountering the terrors of Dame Van Winkle.

As he was about to descend, he heard a voice from a distance, hallooing, " Rip Van Winkle! Rip Van Winkle!" He looked round, but could see nothing but a crow winging its solitary flight across the mountain. He thought his fancy must have deceived him, and turned again to descend, when he heard the same cry ring through the still evening air; " Rip Van Winkle! Rip Van Winkle!"—at the same time Wolf bristled up his back, and, giving a loud growl, skulked to his master's side, looking fearfully down into the glen. Rip now felt a vague apprehension stealing over him; he looked anxiously in the same direction, and perceived a strange figure slowly toiling up the rocks, and bending under the weight of something he carried on his back. He was surprised to see any human being in this lonely and unfrequented place, but supposing it to be some one of the neighbourhood in need of his assistance, he hastened down to yield it.

On nearer approach he was still more surprised at the singularity of the stranger's appearance. He was a short, square-built old fellow, with thick bushy hair and a grizzled beard. His dress was of the antique Dutch fashion—a cloth jerkin, strapped round the waist—several pair of breeches, the outer one of ample volume, decorated with rows of buttons down the sides, and bunches at the knees. He bore on his shoulder a stout keg, that seemed full of liquor, and made signs for Rip to approach and assist him with the load. Though rather shy and distrustful of this new acquaintance, Rip complied with his usual alacrity, and, mutually relieving each other, they clambered up a narrow gully, apparently the dry bed of a mountain torrent. As they ascended, Rip every now and then heard long rolling peals, like distant thunder, that seemed to issue out of a deep ravine, or rather cleft, between lofty rocks, toward which their rugged path conducted. He paused for an instant, but supposing it to be the muttering of one of those transient thunder-showers which often take place in mountain heights, he proceeded. Passing through the ravine, they came to a hollow, like a small amphitheatre, surrounded by perpendicular precipices, over the brinks of which impending trees shot their branches, so that you only caught glimpses of the azure sky and the bright evening cloud. During the whole time Rip and his companion had laboured on in silence, for though the former marvelled greatly what could be the object of carrying a keg of liquor up this wild mountain, yet there was something strange and incomprehensible about the unknown, that inspired awe and checked familiarity.

On entering the amphitheatre, new objects of wonder presented themselves. On a level spot in the centre was a company of odd-looking personages playing at nine-pins. They were dressed in a quaint outlandish fashion; some wore short doublets, others jerkins, with long knives in their belts, and most of them had enormous breeches, of similar style with that of the guide's. Their visages, too, were peculiar: one had a large head, broad face, and small piggish eyes; the face of another seemed to consist entirely of nose, and was surmounted by a white sugar-loaf hat, set off with a little red cock's tail. They all had beards, of various shapes and colours. There was one who seemed to be the commander. He was a stout old gentleman, with a weather-beaten countenance; he wore a laced doublet, broad belt and hanger, high-crowned hat and feather, red stockings, and high-heeled shoes, with roses in them. The whole group reminded Rip of the figures in an old Flemish painting, in the parlour of Dominie Van Shaick, the village parson, and which had been brought over from Holland at the time of the settlement.

What seemed particularly odd to Rip was, that though these folks were evidently amusing themselves, yet they maintained the gravest faces, the most mysterious silence, and were, withal, the most melancholy party of pleasure he had ever witnessed. Nothing interrupted the stillness of the scene but the noise of the balls, which, whenever they were rolled, echoed along the mountains like rumbling peals of thunder.

As Rip and his companion approached them, they suddenly desisted from their play, and stared at him with such fixed, statue-like gaze, and such strange, uncouth, lack-lustre countenances, that his heart turned within him, and his knees smote together. His companion now emptied the contents of the keg into large flagons, and made signs to him to wait upon the company. He obeyed with fear and trembling; they quaffed the liquor in profound silence, and then returned to their game.

By degrees Rip's awe and apprehension subsided. He even ventured, when no eye was fixed upon him, to taste the beverage, which he found had much of the flavour of excellent Hollands. He was naturally a thirsty soul, and was soon tempted to repeat the draught. One taste provoked another; and he reiterated his visits to the flagon so often, that at length his senses were overpowered, his eyes swam in his head, his head gradually declined, and he fell into a deep sleep.

On waking, he found himself on the green knoll whence he had first seen the old man of the glen. He rubbed his eyes—it was a bright sunny morning. The birds were hopping and twittering among the bushes, and the eagle was wheeling aloft, and breasting the pure mountain breeze. "Surely," thought Rip, "I have not slept here all night." He recalled the occurrences before he fell asleep. The strange man with a keg of liquor—the mountain ravine—the wild retreat among the rocks—the woebegone party at nine-pins—the flagon—"Oh! that flagon! that wicked flagon!" thought Rip; "what excuse shall I make to Dame Van Winkle?"

He looked round for his gun, but in place of the clean well-oiled fowling-piece, he found an old firelock lying by him, the barrel incrusted with rust, the lock falling off, and the stock wormeaten. He now suspected that the grave roysters of the mountain had put a trick upon him, and, having dosed him with liquor, had robbed him of his gun. Wolf, too, had disappeared, but he might have strayed away after a squirrel or partridge. He whistled after him, and shouted his name, but all in vain; the echoes repeated his whistle and shout, but no dog was to be seen.

He determined to revisit the scene of the last evening's gambol, and, if he met with any of the party, to demand his dog and gun. As he rose to walk, he found himself stiff in the joints, and wanting in his usual activity. " These mountain beds do not agree with me," thought Rip; " and if this frolic should lay me up with a fit of the rheumatism, I shall have a blessed time with Dame Van Winkle." With some difficulty he got down into the glen: he found the gully up which he and his companion had ascended the preceding evening; but, to his astonishment, a mountain stream was now foaming down it—leaping from rock to rock, and filling the glen with babbling murmurs. He, however, made shift to scramble up its sides, working his toilsome way through thickets of birch, sassafras, and witch-hazel, and sometimes tripped up or entangled by the wild grape-vines that twisted their coils or tendrils from tree to tree, and spread a kind of network in his path.

At length he reached to where the ravine had opened through the cliffs to the amphitheatre; but no traces of such opening remained. The rocks presented a high impenetrable wall, over which the torrent came tumbling in a sheet of feathery foam, and fell into a broad deep basin, black from the shadows of the surrounding forest. Here, then, poor Rip was brought to a stand. He again called and whistled after his dog; he was only answered by the cawing of a flock of idle crows, sporting high in air about a dry tree that overhung a sunny precipice; and who, secure in their elevation, seemed to look down and scoff at the poor man's perplexities. What was to be done?—the morning was passing away, and Rip felt famished for want of his breakfast. He grieved to give up his dog and his gun; he dreaded to meet his wife; but it would not do to starve among the mountains. He shook his head, shouldered the rusty firelock, and, with a heart full of trouble and anxiety, turned his steps homeward.

As he approached the village he met a number of people, but none whom he knew, which somewhat surprised him, for he had thought himself acquainted with every one in the country round. Their dress, too, was of a different fashion from that to which he was accustomed. They all stared at him with equal marks of surprise, and, whenever they cast their eyes upon him, invariably stroked their chins. The constant recurrence of this gesture induced Rip, involuntarily, to do the same —when, to his astonishment, he found his beard had grown a foot long!

He had now entered the skirts of the village. A troop of strange children ran at his heels, hooting after him, and pointing at his grey beard. The dogs, too, not one of which he recognized for an old acquaintance, barked at him as he passed. The very village was altered; it was larger and more populous. There were rows of houses which he had never seen before, and those which had been his familiar haunts had disappeared. Strange names were over the doors—strange faces at the windows —everything was strange. His mind now misgave him; he began to doubt whether both he and the world around him were not bewitched. Surely this was his native village, which he had left but the day before. There stood the Kaatskill mountains—there ran the silver Hudson at a distance—there was every hill and dale precisely as it had always been. Rip was sorely perplexed. " That flagon last night," thought he, " has addled my poor head sadly!"

It was with some difficulty that he found the way to his own house, which he approached with silent awe, expecting every moment to hear the shrill voice of Dame Van Winkle. He found the house gone to decay—the roof fallen in, the windows shattered, and the doors off the hinges. A half-starved dog that looked like Wolf was skulking about it. Rip called him by name, but the cur snarled, showed his teeth, and passed on. This was an unkind cut indeed—" My very dog," sighed poor Rip, " has forgotten me!"

He entered the house, which, to tell the truth, Dame Van Winkle had always kept in neat order. It was empty, forlorn, and apparently abandoned. The desolateness overcame all his connubial fears—he called loudly for his wife and children—the lonely chambers rang for a moment with his voice, and then all again was silence.

He now hurried forth, and hastened to his old resort, the village inn—but it too was gone. A large rickety wooden building stood in its place, with great gaping windows, some of them broken and mended with old hats and petticoats, and over the door was painted, " The Union Hotel, by Jonathan Doolittle ". Instead of the great tree that used to shelter the quiet little Dutch inn of yore, there was now reared a tall naked pole, with something on the top that looked like a red nightcap, and from it was fluttering a flag, on which was a singular assemblage of stars and stripes—all this was strange and incomprehensible. He recognized on the sign, however, the ruby face of King George, under which he had smoked so many a peaceful pipe; but even this was singularly metamorphosed. The red coat was changed for one of blue and buff, a sword was held in the hand instead of a sceptre, the head was decorated with a cocked hat, and underneath was painted in large characters, GENERAL WASHINGTON.

There was, as usual, a crowd of folks about the door, but none that Rip recollected. The very character of the people seemed changed. There was a busy, bustling, disputatious tone about it, instead of the accustomed phlegm and drowsy tranquillity. He looked in vain for the sage Nicholas Vedder, with his broad face, double chin, and fair long pipe, uttering clouds of tobacco-smoke instead of idle speeches; or Van Bummel, the schoolmaster, doling forth the contents of an ancient newspaper. In place of these, a lean, bilious-looking fellow, with his pockets full of handbills, was haranguing vehemently about rights of citizens—elections—members of congress—liberty—Bunker's Hill—heroes of seventy-six—and other words, which were a perfect Babylonish jargon to the bewildered Van Winkle.

The appearance of Rip, with his long grizzled beard, his rusty fowling-piece, his uncouth dress, and an army of women and children at his heels, soon attracted the attention of the tavern politicians. They crowded round him, eyeing him from head to foot with great curiosity.

The orator bustled up to him, and, drawing him partly aside, inquired " on which side he voted?" Rip stared in vacant stupidity. Another short but busy little fellow pulled him by the arm, and, rising on tiptoe, inquired in his ear, " Whether he was Federal of Democrat?" Rip was equally at a loss to comprehend the question; when a knowing, self-important old gentleman, in a sharp cocked hat, made his way through the crowd, putting them to the right and left with his elbows as he passed, and planting himself before Van Winkle, with one arm akimbo, the other resting on his cane, his keen eyes and sharp hat penetrating, as it were, into his very soul, demanded in an austere tone, " What brought him to the election with a gun on his shoulder, and a mob at his heels, and whether he meant to breed a riot in the village?" —" Alas! gentlemen," cried Rip, somewhat dismayed, " I am a poor quiet man, a native of the place, and a loyal subject of the king, God bless him!"

Here a general shout burst from the bystanders—" A tory! a tory! a spy! a refugee! hustle him! away with him!" It was with great difficulty that the self-important man in the cocked hat restored order; and, having assumed a tenfold austerity of brow, demanded again of the unknown culprit what he came there for, and whom he was seeking? The poor man humbly assured him that he meant no harm, but merely came there in search of some of his neighbours, who used to keep about the tavern.

" Well—who are they?—name them."

Rip bethought himself a moment, and inquired, " Where's Nicholas Vedder?"

There was a silence for a little while, when an old man replied in a thin piping voice, " Nicholas Vedder! why, he is dead and gone these eighteen years! There was a wooden tombstone in the churchyard that used to tell all about him, but that's rotten and gone too."

" Where's Brom Dutcher?"

" Oh, he went off to the army in the beginning of the war; some say he was killed at the storming of Stony Point—others say he was drowned in a squall at the foot of Antony's Nose. I don't know—he never came back again."

" Where's Van Bummel, the schoolmaster?"

" He went off to the wars too, was a great militia general, and is now in Congress."

Rip's heart died away at hearing of these sad changes in his home and friends, and finding himself thus alone in the world. Every answer puzzled him too, by treating of such enormous lapses of time, and of matters which he could not understand: war—congress—Stony Point;— he had no courage to ask after any more friends, but cried out in despair, " Does nobody here know Rip Van Winkle?"

" Oh, Rip Van Winkle!" exclaimed two or three. " Oh, to be sure! that's Rip Van Winkle yonder, leaning against the tree."

Rip looked, and beheld a precise counterpart of himself, as he went up the mountain: apparently as lazy, and certainly as ragged. The poor fellow was now completely confounded. He doubted his own identity, and whether he was himself or another man. In the midst of his be-wilderment, the man in the cocked hat demanded who he was, and what was his name?

" God knows," exclaimed he, at his wit's end; " I'm not myself—I'm somebody else—that's me yonder—no —that's somebody else got into my shoes—I was myself last night, but I fell asleep on the mountain, and they've changed my gun, and everything's changed, and I'm changed, and I can't tell what's my name, or who I am!"

The bystanders began now to look at each other, nod, wink significantly, and tap their fingers against their foreheads. There was a whisper, also, about securing the gun, and keeping the old fellow from doing mischief, at the very suggestion of which the self-important man in the cocked hat retired with some precipitation. At this critical moment a fresh comely woman pressed through the throng to get a peep at the grey-bearded man. She had a chubby child in her arms, which, frightened at his looks, began to cry. " Hush, Rip," cried she, " hush, you little fool; the old man won't hurt you." The name of the child, the air of the mother, the tone of her voice, all awakened a train of recollections in his mind.

" What is your name, my good woman?" asked he.

" Judith Gardenier."

" And your father's name?"

" Ah, poor man, Rip Van Winkle was his name, but it's twenty years since he went away from home with his gun, and never has been heard of since—his dog came home without him; but whether he shot himself, or was carried away by the Indians, nobody can tell. I was then but a little girl."

Rip had but one question more to ask; but he put it with a faltering voice:

" Where's your mother?"

" Oh, she too had died but a short time since; she broke a blood-vessel in a fit of passion at a New-England pedlar."

There was a drop of comfort, at least, in this intelli-

gence. The honest man could contain himself no longer.
He caught his daughter and her child in his arms. " I
am your father!" cried he—" Young Rip Van Winkle
once—old Rip Van Winkle now!—Does nobody know
poor Rip Van Winkle?"

All stood amazed, until an old woman, tottering out
from among the crowd, put her hand to her brow, and
peering under it in his face for a moment, exclaimed,
" Sure enough! it is Rip Van Winkle—it is himself!
Welcome home again, old neighbour—Why, where have
you been these twenty long years?"

Rip's story was soon told, for the whole twenty years
had been to him but as one night. The neighbours
stared when they heard it; some were seen to wink at
each other, and put their tongues in their cheeks: and
the self-important man in the cocked hat, who, when the(
alarm was over, had returned to the field, screwed down
the corners of his mouth, and shook his head—upon
which there was a general shaking of the head throughout
the assemblage.

It was determined, however, to take the opinion of old
Peter Vanderdonk, who was seen slowly advancing up
the road. He was a descendant of the historian of that
name, who wrote one of the earliest accounts of the
province. Peter was the most ancient inhabitant of the
village, and well versed in all the wonderful events and
traditions of the neighbourhood. He recollected Rip at
once, and corroborated his story in the most satisfactory
manner. He assured the company that it was a fact,
handed down from his ancestor the historian, that the
Kaatskill mountains had always been haunted by strange
beings. That it was affirmed that the great Hendrick
Hudson, the first discoverer of the river and country,

kept a kind of vigil there every twenty years, with his crew of the *Halfmoon*; being permitted in this way to revisit the scenes of his enterprise, and keep a guardian eye upon the river, and the great city called by his name. That his father had once seen them in their old Dutch dresses playing at nine-pins in a hollow of the mountain, and that he himself had heard, one summer afternoon, the sound of their balls, like distant peals of thunder.

To make a long story short, the company broke up, and returned to the more important concerns of the election. Rip's daughter took him home to live with her; she had a snug, well-furnished house, and a stout cheery farmer for her husband, whom Rip recollected for one of the urchins that used to climb upon his back. As to Rip's son and heir, who was the ditto of himself, seen leaning against the tree, he was employed to work on the farm; but evinced an hereditary disposition to attend to anything else but his business.

Rip now resumed his old walks and habits; he soon found many of his former cronies, though all rather the worse for the wear and tear of time, and preferred making friends among the rising generation, with whom he soon grew into great favour.

Having nothing to do at home, and being arrived at that happy age when a man can be idle with impunity, he took his place once more on the bench at the inn door, and was reverenced as one of the patriarchs of the village, and a chronicle of the old times " before the war ". It was some time before he could get into the regular track of gossip, or could be made to comprehend the strange events that had taken place during his torpor. How that there had been a revolutionary war—that the country had thrown off the yoke of old England—and that, instead of being a subject of his Majesty George the Third, he was now a free citizen of the United States. Rip, in fact, was no politician; the changes of states and empires made but little impression on him; but there was one species of despotism under which he had long groaned, and that was—petticoat government. Happily that was at an end; he had got his neck out of the yoke of matrimony, and could go in and out whenever he pleased without dreading the tyranny of Dame Van Winkle. Whenever her name was mentioned, however, he shook his head, shrugged his shoulders, and cast up his eyes, which might pass either for an expression of resignation to his fate, or joy at his deliverance.

He used to tell his story to every stranger that arrived at Mr. Doolittle's hotel. He was observed at first to vary on some points every time he told it, which was, doubtless, owing to his having so recently awaked. It at last settled down precisely to the tale I have related, and not a man, woman, or child in the neighbourhood but knew it by heart. Some always pretended to doubt the reality of it, and insisted that Rip had been out of his head, and that this was one point on which he always remained flighty. The old Dutch inhabitants, however, almost universally gave it full credit. Even to this day they never hear a thunderstorm of a summer afternoon about the Kaatskill, but they say Hendrick Hudson and his crew are at their game of nine-pins; and it is a common wish of all hen-pecked husbands in the neighbourhood, when life hangs heavy on their hands, that they might have a quieting draught out of Rip Van Winkle's flagon.

S.W. and by W. $\frac{3}{4}$ W.

FREDERICK MARRYAT

Frederick Marryat was born at Westminster in 1792 and died in 1848. At the age of fourteen he entered the navy, and during the next twenty-four years saw active service in many parts of the world. Retiring in 1830, he devoted himself to literary work, and produced a large number of novels, the most famous of which are *Frank Mildmay* (1829), *Peter Simple* (1834), *Mr. Midshipman Easy* (1836), and *Masterman Ready* (1841). Many of his short stories appeared in the *Metropolitan Magazine*, which he edited from 1832 till 1835. Marryat's tales of the sea are among the best of their kind—his own ships, shipmates, and adventures provided him with excellent material, and his work is characterized by directness, realism, and humour.

Jack Littlebrain was, physically considered, as fine grown, and moreover as handsome a boy as ever was seen, but it must be acknowledged that he was not very clever. Nature is, in most instances, very impartial; she has given plumage to the peacock, but, as everyone knows, not the slightest ear for music. Throughout the feathered race it is almost invariably the same; the homeliest clad are the finest songsters. Among animals the elephant is certainly the most intelligent, but, at the same time, he cannot be considered as a beauty. Acting upon this well-ascertained principle, nature imagined that she had done

47

quite enough for Jack when she endowed him with such personal perfection; and did not consider it was at all necessary that he should be very clever; indeed, it must be admitted, not only that he was not very clever, but (as the truth must be told) remarkably dull and stupid. However, the Littlebrains have been for a long while a well-known, numerous, and influential family, so that, if it were possible that Jack could have been taught anything, the means were forthcoming: he was sent to every school in the country; but it was in vain. At every following vacation he was handed over from the one pedagogue to the other, of those whose names were renowned for the Busbian [1] system of teaching by stimulating both ends: he was horsed every day and still remained an ass, and at the end of six months, if he did not run away before that period was over, he was invariably sent back to his parents as incorrigible and unteachable. What was to be done with him? The Littlebrains had always got on in the world, somehow or another, by their interest and connexions; but here was one who might be said to have no brains at all. After many pros and cons, and after a variety of consulting letters had passed between the various members of his family, it was decided that as his maternal uncle, Sir Theophilus Blazers, G.C.B., was at that time second in command in the Mediterranean, he should be sent to sea under his command; the admiral having, in reply to a letter on the subject, answered that it was hard indeed if he did not lick him into some shape or another; and that, at all events, he'd warrant that Jack should be able to box the compass before he had been three months nibbling the

---

[1] The reference is to Dr. Richard Busby (1606–95), headmaster of Westminster School.

ship's biscuit; further, that it was very easy to get over
the examination necessary to qualify him for lieutenant,
as a turkey and a dozen of brown-stout sent in the boat
with him on the passing day, as a present to each of the
passing captains, would pass him, even if he were as in-
competent as a camel (or, as they say at sea, a cable) to
pass through the eye of a needle; that having once passed,
he would soon have him in command of a fine frigate,
with a good nursing first lieutenant; and that if he did
not behave himself properly, he would make his signal to
come on board of the flag-ship, take him into the cabin,
and give him a sound horse-whipping, as other admirals
have been known to inflict upon their own sons under
similar circumstances. The reader must be aware that,
from the tenor of Sir Theophilus' letter, the circumstances
which we are narrating must have occurred some fifty
years ago.

When Jack was informed that he was to be a midshipman, he looked up in the most innocent way in the world
(and innocent he was, sure enough), turned on his heels,
and whistled as he went for want of thought. For the
last three months he had been at home, and his chief
employment was kissing and romping with the maids,
who declared him to be the handsomest Littlebrain that
the country had ever produced. Our hero viewed the
preparations made for his departure with perfect indifference, and wished everybody good-bye with the
utmost composure. He was a happy, good-tempered
fellow, who never calculated, because he could not; never
decided, for he had not wit enough to choose; never fore-
saw, although he could look straight before him; and
never remembered, because he had no memory. The
line, " If ignorance is bliss, 'tis folly to be wise ", was

certainly made especially for Jack; nevertheless he was
not totally deficient: he knew what was good to eat or
drink, for his taste was perfect; his eyes were very sharp,
and he could discover in a moment if a peach was ripe on
the wall; his hearing was quick, for he was the first in
the school to detect the footsteps of his pedagogue; and
he could smell anything savoury nearly a mile off, if
the wind lay the right way. Moreover, he knew that if
he put his fingers in the fire he would burn himself;
that knives cut severely; that birch tickled, and several
other little axioms of this sort which are generally ascer-
tained by children at an early age, but which Jack's capa-
city had not received until at a much later date. Such as
he was, our hero went to sea; his stock in his sea-chest
being very abundant, while his stock of ideas was pro-
portionably small.

We will pass over all the trans-shipments of Jack until
he was eventually shipped on board the *Mendacious*, then
lying at Malta, with the flag of Sir Theophilus Blazers at
the fore—a splendid ship, carrying 120 guns, and nearly
120 midshipmen of different calibres. (I pass over captain,
lieutenant, and ship's company, having made mention of
her most valuable qualifications.) Jack was received with
a hearty welcome by his uncle, for he came in pudding-
time, and was invited to dinner; and the admiral made
the important discovery, that if his nephew was a fool in
other points, he was certainly no fool at his knife and
fork. In a short time his messmates found out that he
was no fool at his fists, and his knock-down arguments
ended much disputation. Indeed, as the French would
say, Jack was perfection in the *physique*, although so very
deficient in the *morale*.

But if Pandora's box proved a plague to the whole

world, Jack had his individual portion of it, when he was
summoned to *box* the compass by his worthy uncle Sir
Theophilus Blazers; who, in the course of six months,
discovered that he could not make his nephew box
it in the three, which he had warranted in his letter;
every day our hero's ears were boxed, but the compass never. It required all the cardinal virtues to teach
him the cardinal points during the forenoon, and he
made a point of forgetting them before the sun went
down. Whenever they attempted it (and various were the
teachers employed to drive the compass into Jack's
head), his head drove round the compass; and try all he
could, Jack never could compass it. It appeared, as some
people are said only to have one idea, as if Jack could
only have one *point* in his head at a time, and to that
point he would stand like a well-broken pointer. With
him the wind never changed till the next day. His
uncle pronounced him to be a fool, but that did not
hurt his nephew's feelings; he had been told so too often
already.

I have said that Jack had a great respect for good
eating and drinking, and, moreover, was blessed with a
good appetite: every person has his peculiar fancies, and
if there was anything which more titillated the palate
and olfactory nerves of our hero, it was a roast goose with
sage and onions. Now it so happened, that having been
about seven months on board of the *Mendacious*, Jack
had one day received a summons to dine with the admiral,
for the steward had ordered a roast goose for dinner, and
knew not only that Jack was partial to it, but also that
Jack was the admiral's nephew, which always goes for
something on board of a flag-ship. Just before they were
sitting down to table, the admiral wishing to know how

the wind was, and having been not a little vexed with the slow progress of his nephew's nautical acquirements, said, " Now, Mr. Littlebrain, go up and bring me down word how the wind is; and mark me, as, when you are sent, nine times out of ten you make a mistake, I shall now bet you five guineas against your dinner, that you make a mistake this time: so now be off and we will soon ascertain whether you lose your dinner or I lose my money. Sit down, gentlemen, we will not wait for Mr. Littlebrain."

Jack did not much admire this bet on the part of his uncle, but still less did he like the want of good manners in not waiting for him. He had just time to see the covers removed, to scent a whiff of the goose, and was off.

" The admiral wants to know how the wind is, sir," said Jack to the officer of the watch.

The officer of the watch went to the binnacle, and setting the wind as nearly as he could, replied, " Tell Sir Theophilus that it is *S.W. and by W.* $\frac{3}{4}$ *W.*"

" That's one of those confounded long points that I never can remember," cried Jack, in despair.

" Then you'll ' get goose ', as the saying is," observed one of the midshipmen.

" No; I'm afraid that I shan't get any," replied Jack, despondingly. " What did he say, S.W. and by N. $\frac{3}{4}$ E.?"

" Not exactly," replied his messmate, who was a good-natured lad, and laughed heartily at Jack's version. " S.W. and by W. $\frac{3}{4}$ W."

" I never can remember it," cried Jack. " I'm to have five guineas if I do, and no dinner if I don't; and if I stay here much longer, I shall get no dinner at all events, for they are all terribly peckish, and there will be none left."

" Well, if you'll give me one of the guineas, I'll show you how to manage it," said the midshipman.

" I'll give you two, if you'll only be quick and the goose a'n't all gone," replied Jack.

The midshipman wrote down the point from which the wind blew, at full length, upon a bit of paper, and pinned it to the rim of Jack's hat. " Now," said he, " when you go into the cabin, you can hold your hat so as to read it without their perceiving you."

" Well, so I can; I never should have thought of that," said Jack.

" You hav'n't wit enough," replied the midshipman.

" Well, I see no wit in the compass," replied Jack.

" Nevertheless, it's full of point," replied the midshipman: " now be quick."

Our hero's eyes served him well if his memory was treacherous; and as he entered the cabin door he bowed over his hat very politely, and said, as he read it off, " S.W. and by W. ¾ W.," and then he added, without reading at all, " if you please, Sir Theophilus."

" Steward," said the admiral, " tell the officer of the watch to step down."

" How's the wind, Mr. Growler?"

" S.W. and by W. ¾ W.," replied the officer.

" Then, Mr. Littlebrain, you have won your five guineas, and may now sit down and enjoy your dinner."

Our hero was not slow in obeying the order, and ventured, upon the strength of his success, to send his plate twice for goose. Having eaten their dinner, drunk their wine, and taken their coffee, the officers, at the same time, took the hint which invariably accompanies the latter beverage, made their bows and retreated. As Jack was following his seniors out of the cabin, the admiral put the sum which he had staked into his hands, observing, that " it was an ill wind that blew nobody good."

So thought Jack, who, having faithfully paid the midshipman the two guineas for his assistance, was now on the poop keeping his watch, as midshipmen usually do; that is, stretched out on the signal lockers and composing himself to sleep after the most approved fashion, answering the winks of the stars by blinks of his eyes, until at last he shut them to keep them warm. But, before he had quite composed himself, he thought of the goose and the five guineas. The wind was from the same quarter, blowing soft and mild; Jack lay in a sort of reverie, as it fanned his cheek, for the weather was close and sultry.

" Well," muttered Jack to himself, " I do love that point of the compass, at all events, and I think that I never shall forget S.W. and by W. $\frac{3}{4}$ W. No I never— never liked one before, though——"

" Is that true?" whispered a gentle voice in his ear; " do you love ' S.W. and by W. $\frac{3}{4}$ W.', and will you, as you say, never forget her?"

" Why, what's that?" said Jack, opening his eyes and turning half round on his side.

" It's me—' S.W. and by W. $\frac{3}{4}$ W.', that you say you love."

Littlebrain raised himself and looked round;—there was no one on the poop except himself and two or three of the after-guard, who were lying down between the guns.

" Why, who was it that spoke?" said Jack, much astonished.

" It was the wind you love and who has long loved

you," replied the same voice; "do you wish to see me?"

"See you—see the wind?—I've been already sent on that message by the midshipmen," thought Jack.

"Do you love me as you say, and as I love you?" continued the voice.

"Well, I like you better than any other point of the compass, and I'm sure I never thought I should like one of them," replied Jack.

"That will not do for me; will you love only me?"

"I'm not likely to love the others," replied Jack, shutting his eyes again; "I *hate* them all."

"And love me?"

"Well, I do love you, that's a fact," replied Jack, as he thought of the goose and the five guineas.

"Then look round and you shall see me," said the soft voice.

Jack, who hardly knew whether he was asleep or awake, did at this summons once more take the trouble to open his eyes, and beheld a fairy female figure, pellucid as water, yet apparently possessing substance; her features were beautifully soft and mild, and her outline trembled and shifted as it were, waving gently to and fro. It smiled sweetly, hung over him, played with his chestnut curls, softly touched his lips with her own, passed her trembling fingers over his cheeks, and its warm breath appeared as if it melted into his. Then it grew more bold, —embraced his person, searched into his neck and collar, as if curious to examine him.

Jack felt a pleasure and gratification which he could not well comprehend: once more the charmer's lips trembled upon his own, now remaining for a moment, now withdrawing, again returning to kiss and kiss again, and once more did the soft voice put the question,—

"Do you love me?"

"Better than goose," replied Jack.

"I don't know who goose may be," replied the fairy form, as she tossed about Jack's waving locks; "you must love only me, promise me that before I am relieved."

"What, have you got the first watch, as well as me?" replied Jack.

"I am on duty just now, but I shall not be so long. We southerly winds are never kept long in one place; some of my sisters will probably be sent here soon."

"I don't understand what you talk about," replied Jack. "Suppose you tell me who you are, and what you are, and I'll do all I can to keep awake; I don't know how it is, but I've felt more inclined to go to sleep since you have been fanning me about, than I did before."

"Then I will remain by your side while you listen to me. I am, as I told you, a wind——"

"That's puzzling," said Jack, interrupting her.

"My name is ' S.W. and by W. $\frac{3}{4}$ W.'."

"Yes, and a very long name it is. If you wish me to remember you, you should have had a shorter one."

This ruffled the wind a little, and she blew rather sharp into the corner of Jack's eye,—however she proceeded,—

"You are a sailor, and of course you know all the winds on the compass by name."

"I wish I did; but I don't," replied Littlebrain; "I can recollect you, and not one other."

Again the wind trembled with delight on his lips, and she proceeded:—"You know that there are thirty-two points on the compass, and these points are divided into quarters; so that there are, in fact, 128 different winds."

" There are more than I could ever remember; I know that," said Jack.

" Well, we are in all 128. All the winds which have northerly in them are coarse and ugly; all the southern winds are pretty."

" You don't say so?" replied our hero.

" We are summoned to blow, as required, but the hardest duty generally falls to the northerly winds, as it should do, for they are the strongest; although we southerly winds can blow hard enough when we choose. Our characters are somewhat different. The most unhappy in disposition, and I may say the most malevolent, are the north and easterly winds; the N.W. winds are powerful, but not unkind; the S.E. winds vary, but, at all events, we of the S.W. are considered the mildest and the most beneficent. Do you understand me?"

" Not altogether. You're going right round the compass, and I never could make it out, that's a fact. I hear what you say, but I cannot promise to recollect it; I can only recollect S.W. and by W. ¾ W."

" I care only for your recollecting me; if you do that, you may forget all the rest. Now you see we South Wests are summer winds, and are seldom required but in this season; I have often blown over your ship these last three months, and I always have lingered near you, for I loved you."

" Thank you—now go on, for seven bells have struck some time, and I shall be going to turn in. Is your watch out?"

" No, I shall blow for some hours longer. Why will you leave me—why won't you stay on deck with me?"

"What, stay on deck after my watch is out? No, if I do, blow me! We midshipmen never do that—but I say, why can't you come down with me, and talk to me before I turn in. My hammock is close to the hatchway, and you can easily do it."

"Well, I will, upon one promise. You say that you love me, now I'm very jealous, for we winds are always supplanting one another. Promise me that you will never mention any other wind in the compass but me, for if you do, they may come to you, and if I hear of it I'll blow the masts out of your ship, that I will."

"You don't say so?" replied Jack, surveying her fragile, trembling form.

"Yes, I will, and on a lee-shore too; so that the ship shall go to pieces on the rocks, and the admiral and every soul on board her be drowned."

"No, you wouldn't, would you?" said our hero, astonished.

"Not if you promise me. Then I'll come to you and pour down your windsails, and dry your washed clothes as they hang on the rigging, and just ripple the waves as you glide along, and hang upon the lips of my dear love, and press him in my arms. Promise me, then, on no account ever to recollect or mention any other wind but me."

"Well, I think I may promise that," replied Jack, "I'm very clever at forgetting; and then you'll come, won't you, and keep me company?"

"Yes, I'll watch you while you sleep, and I'll fan your cheeks, and keep you cool and comfortable, till I'm relieved."

"And when you go, when will you come again?"

"That I cannot tell—when I'm summoned; and I

shall wait with impatience, that you may be sure of."

"There's eight bells," said Jack, starting up; "I must go down and call the officer of the middle watch; but I'll soon turn in, for my relief is not so big as myself, and I can thrash him."

Littlebrain was as good as his word; he cut down his relief, and then thrashed him for venturing to expostulate. The consequence was, that in ten minutes he was in his hammock, and "S.W. and by W. ¾ W." came gently down the hatchway and breathed softly on his cheeks. Jack soon fell fast asleep, and when he was wakened up the next morning by the quarter-master, she was no longer there. A mate inquiring how the wind was, was answered by the quarter-master that they had a fresh breeze from the N.N.W., by which Jack understood that his sweetheart was no longer on duty.

Our hero now could think of nothing else but his kind companion; he longed for her to come again, and, to the surprise of everybody, was now perpetually making inquiries as to the wind which blew. He thought of her continually; and in fact was as much in love with "S.W. and by W. ¾ W." as he possibly could be. She came again and again and talked to him while he was on deck, and blew softly upon him while he slept. But she had always to go when relieved by another.

We do not intend to accuse the wind of inconstancy, as that was not her fault; nor of treachery, for she loved dearly; nor of violence, for she was all softness and mildness; but we do say that "S.W. and by W. ¾ W." was the occasion of Jack being very often in a scrape, for our hero kept his word; he forgot all other winds, and with him there was no other except his dear "S.W. and by W. ¾ W.". It must be admitted of Jack, that, at all events, he showed great perseverance, for he stuck to his point.

Our hero would argue with his messmates, for it is not those who are most capable of arguing who are most fond of it; and, like all arguers not very brilliant, he would flounder and diverge away right and left, just as the flaws of ideas came into his head.

" What nonsense it is your talking that way," would his opponent say; " why don't you come to the point?"

" And so I do," cried Jack.

" Well, then, what is your point?"

" S.W. and by W. $\frac{3}{4}$ W.," replied our hero.

Who could reply to this? But in every instance, and through every difficulty, our hero kept his promise, until his uncle, Sir Theophilus, was very undecided whether he should send him home to be locked up in a lunatic asylum, or bring him on in the service to the rank of post-captain. Upon mature consideration, however, as a man in Bedlam is a very useless member of society, and a teetotal non-productive, whereas a captain in the navy is a responsible agent, the admiral came to the conclusion that Littlebrain must follow up his destiny.

At last Jack was set down as the greatest fool in the ship, and was pointed out as such. The ladies observed that such might possibly be the case, but at all events he was the handsomest young man in the Mediterranean fleet. We believe that both parties were correct in their assertions.

Time flies—even a midshipman's time, which does not fly quite so fast as his money—and the time came for Mr. Littlebrain's examination. Sir Theophilus, who now commanded the whole fleet, was almost in despair. How was it possible that a man could navigate a ship with only one quarter point of the compass in his head?

Sir Theophilus scratched his wig; and the disposition of the Mediterranean fleet, so important to the country, was altered according to the dispositions of the captains who commanded the ships. In those days there were martinets in the service; officers who never overlooked an offence, or permitted the least deviation from strict duty; who were generally hated, but at the same time were most valuable to the service. As for his nephew passing his examination before any of those of the first or second, or even of the third degree, the admiral knew that it was impossible. The consequence was, that one was sent away on a mission to Genoa about nothing; another to watch for vessels never expected, off Sardinia; two more to cruise after a French frigate which had never been built: and thus, by degrees, did the admiral arrange, so as to obtain a set of officers sufficiently pliant to allow his nephew to creep under the gate which barred his promotion, and which he never could have vaulted over. So the signal was made—our hero went on board—his uncle had not forgotten the propriety of a little *douceur* on the occasion; and, as the turkeys were all gone, three couple of geese were sent in the same boat, as a present to each of the three passing captains. Littlebrain's heart failed him as he pulled to the ship; even the geese hissed at him, as much as to say, " If you were not such a stupid ass, we might have been left alive in our coops." There was a great deal of truth in that remark, if they did say so.

Nothing could have been made more easy for Little-brain than his examination. The questions had all been arranged beforehand; and some kind friend had given him all the answers written down. The passing captains apparently suffered from the heat of the weather, and each had his hand on his brow, looking down on the table at the time that Littlebrain gave his answers, so that of course they did not observe that he was reading them off. As soon as Littlebrain had given his answer, and had had sufficient time to drop his paper under the table, the captains felt better and looked up again.

There were but eight questions for our hero to answer. Seven had been satisfactorily got through; then came the eighth, a very simple one: "What is your course and distance from Ushant to the Start?" This question having been duly put, the captains were again in deep meditation, shrouding their eyes with the palms of their hands.

Littlebrain had his answer—he looked at the paper. What could be more simple than to reply?—and then the captains would have all risen up, shaken him by the hand, complimented him upon the talent he had displayed, sent their compliments to the commander-in-chief, and their thanks for the geese. Jack was just answering, " North——"

" Recollect your promise!" cried a soft voice, which Jack well recollected.

Jack stammered—the captains were mute—and waited patiently.

" I must say it," muttered Jack.

" You shan't," replied the little Wind.

" Indeed I must," said Jack, " or I shall be turned back."

The captains, surprised at this delay and the muttering of Jack, looked up, and one of them gently inquired if Mr. Littlebrain had not dropped his handkerchief or

something under the table? And then they again fixed
their eyes upon the green cloth.

"If you dare, I'll never see you again," cried "S.W.
and by W. ¾ W."—"never come to you—but I'll blow
the ship on shore, every soul shall be lost, admiral and
all; recollect your promise!"

"Then I shall never pass," replied Jack.

"Do you think that any other point in the compass
shall pass you except me?—never! I am too jealous for
that. Come now, dearest!" and the Wind again deliciously
trembled upon the lips of our hero, who could no longer
resist.

"S.W. and by W. ¾ W.," exclaimed Jack firmly.

"You have made a slight mistake, Mr. Littlebrain,"
said one of the captains. "*Look* again—I meant to say,
think again."

"S.W. and by W. ¾ W.," again repeated Jack.

"Dearest, how I love you!" whispered the soft Wind.

"Why, Mr. Littlebrain," said one of the captains—for
Jack had actually laid the paper down on the table—
"what's in the wind now?"

"She's obstinate," replied Jack.

"You appear to be so, at all events," replied the
captain. "Pray, try once more."

"I have it!" thought Jack, who tore off the last answer
from his paper. "I gained five guineas by that plan once
before." He then handed the bit of paper to the passing
captain: "I believe that's right, sir," said our hero.

"Yes, that is right; but could you not have said it
instead of writing it, Mr. Littlebrain?"

Jack made no reply; his little sweetheart pouted a
little, but said nothing; it was an evasion which she did
not like. A few seconds of consultation then took place,

as a matter of form. Each captain asked of the other if he was perfectly satisfied as to Mr. Littlebrain's capabilities, and the reply was in the affirmative; and they were perfectly satisfied that he was either a fool or a madman. However, as we have had both in the service by way of precedent, Jack was added to the list, and the next day was appointed lieutenant.

Our hero did his duty as lieutenant of the forecastle; and as all the duty of that officer is, when hailed from the quarter-deck, to answer, "*Ay, ay, sir,*" he got on without making many mistakes. And now he was very happy; no one dared to call him a fool except his uncle; he had his own cabin, and many was the time that his dear little " S.W. and by W. ¾ W." would come in by the scuttle and nestle by his side.

" You won't see so much of me soon, dearest," said she, one morning, gravely.

" Why not, my soft one?" replied Jack.

" Don't you recollect that the winter months are coming on?"

" So they are," replied Jack. " Well, I shall long for you back."

And Jack did long, and long very much, for he loved his dear wind and the fine weather which accompanied her. Winter came on, and heavy gales and rain, and thunder and lightning; nothing but double-reefed topsails and wearing in succession; and our hero walked the forecastle and thought of his favourite wind. The N.E. winds came down furiously, and the weather was bitter cold. The officers shook the rain and spray off their garments when their watch was over, and called for grog.

" Steward, a glass of grog," cried one; " and let it be strong."

" The same for me," said Jack; " only, I'll mix it myself."

Jack poured out the rum till the tumbler was half full.

" Why, Littlebrain," said his messmate, " that is a dose; that's what we call a regular *Nor-wester*."

" Is it?" replied Jack. " Well, then, Nor-westers suit me exactly, and I shall stick to them like cobblers' wax."

And during the whole of the winter months our hero showed a great predilection for Nor-westers.

It was in the latter end of February that there was a heavy gale; it had blown furiously from the northward for three days, and then it paused and panted as if out of breath—no wonder! And then the wind shifted and shifted again, with squalls and heavy rain, until it blew from every quarter of the compass.

Our hero's watch was over, and he came down and called for a " Nor-wester " as usual.

" How is the wind now?" asked the first lieutenant of the master, who came down dripping wet.

" S.S.W., but drawing now fast to the westward," said old Spunyarn.

And so it was; and it veered round until " S.W. and by W. ¾ W.", with an angry gust, came down the skylight, and blowing strongly into our hero's ear, cried—

" Oh, you false one!"

" False!" exclaimed Jack. " What! you here, and so angry too? What's the matter?"

" What's the matter!—do you think I don't know? What have you been doing ever since I was away, comforting yourself during my absence with *Nor-westers*?"

" Why, you an't jealous of a Nor-wester, are you?"

replied Littlebrain. " I confess I'm rather partial to them."

" What!—this to my face!—I'll never come again, unless you promise me that you will have nothing to do with them, and never call for one again. Be quick— I cannot stay more than two minutes; for it is hard work now, and we relieve quick—say the word."

" Well, then," replied Littlebrain, " you've no objection to *half-and-half*?"

" None in the world; that's quite another thing, and has nothing to do with the wind."

" It has though," thought Jack, " for it gets a man in the wind; but I won't tell her so; and," continued he, " you don't mind a raw nip, do you?"

" No—I care for nothing except a Nor-wester."

" I'll never call for one again," replied Jack; " it is but making my grog a little stronger; in future it shall be *half-and-half*."

" That's a dear! Now I'm off—don't forget me;" and away went the wind in a great hurry.

It was about three months after this short visit, the fleet being off Corsica, that our hero was walking the deck, thinking that he soon should see the object of his affections, when a privateer brig was discovered at anchor a few miles from Bastia. The signal was made for the boats of the fleet to cut her out; and the admiral, wishing that his nephew should distinguish himself somehow, gave him the command of one of the finest boats. Now Jack was as brave as brave could be; he did not know what danger was; he hadn't wit enough to perceive it, and there was no doubt but he would distinguish himself. The boats went on the service. Jack was the very first on board, cheering his men as he darted into the closed ranks of his opponents. Whether it was that he did not think that his head was worth defending, or that he was too busy in breaking the heads of others to look after his own, this is certain, that a tomahawk descended upon it with such force as to bury itself in his skull (and his was a thick skull too). The privateer's men were overpowered by numbers, and then our hero was discovered, under a pile of bodies, still breathing heavily. He was hoisted on board and taken into his uncle's cabin: the surgeon shook his head when he had examined that of our hero.

" It must have been a most tremendous blow," said he to the admiral, " to have penetrated——"

" It must have been, indeed," replied the admiral, as the tears rolled down his cheeks; for he loved his nephew.

The surgeon having done all that his art would enable him to do, left the cabin to attend to the others who were hurt; the admiral also went on the quarter-deck, walking to and fro for an hour in a melancholy mood. He returned to the cabin and bent over his nephew; Jack opened his eyes.

" My dear fellow," said the admiral, " how's your head now?"

" S.W. and by W. ¾ W.," faintly exclaimed our hero, constant in death, as he turned a little on one side and expired.

It was three days afterwards, as the fleet were on a wind making for Malta, that the bell of the ship tolled, and a body, sewed up in a hammock and covered with the Union Jack, was carried to the gangway by the admiral's bargemen. It had been a dull, cloudy day, with little wind; the hands were turned up, the officers and men stood uncovered; the admiral in advance with his arms folded, as the chaplain read the funeral service over the body of our hero,—and as the service proceeded, the sails flapped, for the wind had shifted a little; a motion was made, by the hand of the officer of the watch, to the man at the helm to let the ship go off the wind, that the service might not be disturbed, and a mizzling soft rain descended. The wind had shifted to our hero's much-loved *point*; his fond mistress had come to mourn over the loss of her dearest, and the rain that descended were the tears which she shed at the death of her handsome but not over-gifted lover.

Paddy the Piper

SAMUEL LOVER

Samuel Lover was born in Dublin in 1797 and died in 1868. He was a man of great versatility, and became distinguished as a painter of miniatures and portraits, as a song writer, and as a novelist. In 1831 he published his first book, *Legends and Stories of Ireland*, and in 1837 his first novel, *Rory O'More*, appeared. *Handy Andy*, his best-known book, was published in 1842. Lover's short stories, many of which were contributed to Dublin periodicals, are, like his novels, characteristically Irish in their rollicking humour. *Paddy the Piper* is a tale of 1798 when Ireland rose in rebellion to secure religious and political freedom. The country was placed under martial law, and people who went out of doors after nightfall ran a serious risk of being shot without warning by Government soldiers.

I'll tell you, sir, a mighty quare story, and it's as thrue as I'm standin' here, and that's no lie:—It was in the time of the *'ruction*[1], whin the long summer days, like many a fine fellow's precious life, was cut short by raison of the martial law,—that wouldn't let a dacent boy be out in the evenin', good or bad; for whin the day's work was over, divil a one of uz daar go to meet a frind over a glass, or a girl at the dance, but must go home, and shut ourselves up, and never budge, nor rise latch, nor dhraw boult antil the morning kem agin.

[1] Insurrection.
69

Well, to come to my story:—'Twas afther nightfall,
and we wor sittin' round the fire, and the pratees was
boilin', and the noggins of butther-milk was standing
ready for our suppers, whin a knock kem to the door.
"Whisht," says my father, "here's the sojers come upon
us now," says he; "bad luck to thim the villians, I'm
afeard they seen a glimmer of the fire through the crack
in the door," says he. "No," says my mother, "for I'm
afther hanging an ould sack and my new petticoat agin
it, a while ago." "Well, whisht, any how," says my father,
"for there's a knock agin;" and we all held our tongues
till another thump kem to the door. "Oh, it's folly to
purtind any more," says my father—"they're too cute to
be put off that-a-way," says he. "Go, Shamus," says he
to me, "and see who's in it." "How can I see who's in it
in the dark?" says I. "Well," says he, "light the candle
thin, and see who's in it, but don't open the door for
your life, barrin' they break it in," says he, "exceptin' to
the sojers, and spake thim fair, if it's thim."

So with that I wint to the door, and there was another
knock. "Who's there?" says I. "It's me," says he. "Who
are you?" says I. "A frind," says he. "*Baithershin*," says
I, "who are you at all?" "Arrah! don't you know me?"
says he. "Divil a taste," says I. "Sure I'm Paddy the
piper," says he. "Oh, thundher and turf," says I, "is it
you, Paddy, that's in it?" "Sorra one else," says he.
"And what brought you at this hour?" says I. "By gar,"
says he, "I didn't like goin' the roun' by the road," says
he, "and so I kem the short cut, and that's what delayed
me," says he. "Oh, bloody wars!" says I—"Paddy, I
wouldn't be in your shoes for the king's ransom," says
I; "for you know yourself it's a hanging matther to be
cotched out these times," says I. "Sure I know that,"

says he, " God help me; and that's what I kem to you
for," says he; " and let me in for old acquaintance sake,"
says poor Paddy. " Oh, by this and that," says I, " I
darn't open the door for the wide world; and sure you
know it; and troth if the Husshians[1] or the Yeo's[2] ketches
you," says I—" they'll murther you, as sure as your
name's Paddy." " Many thanks to you," says he, " for
your good intintions; but, plaze the pigs, I hope it's not
the likes o' that is in store for me, any how." " Faix
then," says I, " you had betther lose no time in hidin'
yourself," says I; " for throth I tell you, it's a short thrial
and a long rope the Husshians would be afther givin'
you—for they've no justice, and less marcy, the villians!"
" Faith thin, more's the raison you should let me in,
Shamus," says poor Paddy. " It's a folly to talk," says I,
" I darn't open the door." " Oh, then, millia murther!"
says Paddy, " what'll become of me at all, at all," says
he. " Go aff into the shed," says I, " behind the house,
where the cow is, and there there's an illigant lock o'
straw, that you may go sleep in," says I, " and a fine bed
it id be for a lord, let alone a piper."

So off Paddy set to hide in the shed, and throth it
wint to our hearts to refuse him, and turn him away
from the door, more, by token, when the pratees was
ready—for sure the bit and the sup is always welkim to
the poor thraveller. Well, we all wint to bed, and Paddy
hid himself in the cow-house; and now I must tell you
how it was with Paddy:—You see, afther sleeping for
some time, Paddy wakened up, thinkin' it was mornin',
but it wasn't mornin' at all, but only the light o' the
moon that deceaved him; but at all evints, he wanted to

---

[1] Hessians.　　　[2] Yeomen.

be stirring airly, bekase he was goin' off to the town hard
by, it bein' fair-day, to pick up a few ha'pence with his
pipes—for the divil a betther piper was in all the country
round, nor Paddy; and every one gave it up to Paddy,
that he was illigant on the pipes, and played " Jinny
bang'd the Weaver ", beyant tellin', and the " Hare in
the Corn ", that you'd think the very dogs was in it,
and the horsemen ridin' like mad.

Well, as I was sayin', he set off to go to the fair, and
he wint meandherin' along through the fields, but he
didn't go far, antil climbin' up through a hedge, when
he was comin' out at t'other side, his head kem plump
agin somethin' that made the fire flash out iv his eyes.
So with that he looks up—and what do you think it was,
Lord be marciful unto uz, but a corpse hangin' out of a
branch of a three. " Oh, the top of the mornin' to you,
sir," says Paddy, " and is that the way with you, my poor
fellow? throth you took a start out o' me," says poor
Paddy; and 'twas thrue for him, for it would make the
heart of a stouter man nor Paddy jump, to see the like,
and to think of a Christhan crathur being hanged up, all
as one as a dog.

Now 'twas the rebels that hanged this chap—bekase,
you see, the corpse had got clothes an him, and that's the
raison that one might know it was the rebels—by rayson
that the Husshians and the Orangemen never hanged
anybody wid good clothes an him, but only the poor and
definceless crathurs, like uz; so, as I said before, Paddy
knew well it was the *boys*[1] that done it; " and," says
Paddy, eyein' the corpse, " by my soul, thin, but you have
a beautiful pair of boots an you," says he, " and it's what

---

[1] That is, the rebels.

I'm thinkin' you won't have any great use for thim no more; and sure it's a shame to see the likes o' me," says he, " the best piper in the sivin counties, to be trampin' wid a pair of ould brogues not worth three *traneens*[1], and a corpse wid such an illigant pair o' boots, that wants some one to wear thim." So, with that, Paddy lays hould of him by the boots, and began a pullin' at thim, but they wor mighty stiff; and whether it was by rayson of their being so tight, or the branch of the three a-jiggin' up and down, all as one as a weighdee buckettee, and not lettin' Paddy cotch any right hoult o' thim—he could get no *advantage* o' thim at all—and at last he gev it up, and was goin' away, whin looking behind him agin, the sight of the illigant fine boots was too much for him, and he turned back, determined to have the boots, anyhow, by fair means or foul; and I'm loath to tell you now how he got thim—for indeed it was a dirty turn, and throth it was the only dirty turn I ever knew Paddy to be guilty av; and you see it was this-a-way: 'pon my sowl, he pulled out a big knife, and by the same token, it was a knife with a fine buck-handle, and a murtherin' big blade, that an uncle o' mine, that was a gardener at the lord's, made Paddy a prisint av; and more by token, it was not the first mischief that knife done, for it cut love between thim, that was the best of friends before; and sure 'twas the wondher of every one, that two knowledgeable men, that ought to know betther, would do the likes, and give and take sharp steel in friendship; but I'm forgettin'— well, he outs with his knife, and what does he do, but he cut off the legs av the corpse; " and," says he, " I can take aff the boots at my convaynience;" and throth it was, as I said before, a dirty turn.

[1] Blades of grass.

Well, sir, he tuck'd up the legs undher his arm, and at
that minit the moon peeped out from behind a cloud—
" Oh! is it there you are?" says he to the moon, for he was
an impident chap—and thin, seein' that he made a mistake,
and that the moonlight deceaved him, and that it wasn't
the airly dawn, as he conceaved; and bein' friken'd for
fear himself might be cotched and trated like the poor
corps he was afther malthreating, if *he* was found walking
the counthry at that time—by gar, he turned about, and
walked back agin to the cow-house, and, hidin' the corps's
legs in the sthraw, Paddy wint to sleep agin. But what
do you think? the divil a long Paddy was there antil the
sojers kem in airnest, and, by the powers, they carried off
Paddy—and 'faith it was only sarvin' him right for what
he done to the poor corps.

Well, whin the morning kem, my father says to me,
" Go, Shamus," says he, " to the shed, and bid poor
Paddy come in, and take share o' the pratees, for I go
bail he's ready for his breakquest by this, anyhow."

Well, out I wint to the cow-house, and called out
" Paddy!" and afther callin' three or four times, and
gettin' no answer, I wint in, and called agin, and divil
an answer I got still. " Blood-an-agers!" says I, " Paddy,
where are you, at all, at all?" and so castin' my eyes about
the shed, I seen two feet sticking out from undher the
hape o' sthraw—" Musha! thin," says I, " bad luck to
you, Paddy, but you're fond of a warm corner, and maybe
you haven't made yourself as snug as a flay in a blanket?
but I'll disturb your dhrames, I'm thinkin'," says I, and
with that I laid hould of his heels (as I thought, God
help me), and givin' a good pull to waken him, as I
intindid, away I wint, head over heels, and my brains
was a'most knocked out agin the wall.

Well, whin I recovered myself, there I was, an the broad o' my back, and two things stickin' out o' my hands, like a pair o' Husshian's horse-pistils—and I thought the sight 'id lave my eyes, whin I seen they were two mortial legs. My jew'l, I threw them down like a hot pratee, and jumpin' up, I roared out millia murther. "Oh, you murtherin' villian," says I, shaking my fist at the cow—" Oh, you unnath'ral *baste*," says I, " you've ate poor Paddy, you thievin' cannable, you're worse than a neyger," says I; " and bad luck to you, how dainty you are, that nothin' 'id serve you for your supper but the best piper in Ireland? *Weirasthru! weirasthru!* what'll the whole counthry say to such an unnath'ral murther? and you, lookin' as innocent there as a lamb, and eating your hay, as quiet as if nothin' happened."—With that, I ran out, for throth I didn't like to be near her; and goin' in to the house, I tould them all about it.

"Arrah! be aisy," says my father. " Bad luck to the lie I tell you," says I. " Is it ate Paddy?" says they. " Divil a doubt of it," says I. " Are you sure, Shamus?" says my mother. " I wish I was as sure of a new pair o' brogues," says I. " Bad luck to the bit she has left iv him, but his two legs." " And do you tell me she ate the pipes too?" says my father. " By gor, I b'lieve so," says I. " Oh, the divil fly away wid her," says he, " what a cruel taste she has for music!" " Arrah!" says my mother, " don't be cursing the cow that gives the milk to the childher." " Yis, I will," says my father; " why shouldn't I curse sitch an unnath'ral baste?" " You oughtn't to curse any livin' that's undher your roof," says my mother. " By my sowl, thin," says my father, " she shan't be undher my roof any more; for I'll sind her to the fair this minit," says he, " and sell her for whatever she'll bring. Go aff," says he, " Shamus, the minit you've ate your breakquest, and dhrive her to the fair." " Throth, I don't like to dhrive her," says I. " Arrah, don't be makin' a gommagh of yourself," says he. " Faith, I don't," says I. " Well, like or no like," says he, " you must dhrive her." " Sure, father," says I, " you could take more care of her yourself." " That's mighty good," says he, " to keep a dog and bark myself;" and faith I rec'llected the sayin' from that hour—" let me have no more words about it," says he, " but be aff wid you."

So, aff I wint, and it's no lie I'm tellin', whin I say it was sore agin my will I had anything to do with sitch a villian of a baste. But, howsomever, I cut a brave long wattle, that I might dhrive the man-ather iv a thief, as she was, without bein' near her at all, at all.

Well, away we wint along the road, and mighty throng it wuz wid the boys and the girls, and, in short, all sorts, rich and poor, high and low, crowdin' to the fair.

" God save you," says one to me. " God save you, kindly," says I. " That's a fine baste you're dhrivin'," says he. " Throth, she is," says I; though God knows it wint agin my heart to say a good word for the likes of her. " It's to the fair you're goin', I suppose," says he, " with the baste?" (He was a snug-lookin' farmer, ridin' a purty little grey hack.) " Faith, thin, you're right enough," says I, " it is to the fair I'm goin'." " What do you expec' for her," says he. " Faith, thin, myself doesn't know," says I—and that was thrue enough, you see, bekase I was bewildered like, about the baste, intirely. " That's a quare way to be goin' to market," says he, " and not to know what you expec' for your baste." " Och," says I—not likin' to let him suspect there was anything wrong wid her—" Och," says I, in a careless

sort of a way, " sure no one can tell what a baste 'll bring,
antil they come to the fair," says I, " and see what price
is goin'." " Indeed, that's nath'ral enough," says he.
" But if you wor bid a fair price before you come to the
fair, sure you might as well take it," says he. " Oh, I've
no objection in life," says I. " Well thin, what will you
ax for her?" says he. " Why thin, I wouldn't like to be
onraysonable," says I—(for the thruth was, you know,
I wanted to get rid iv her)—" and so I'll take four pounds
for her," says I, " and *no less*." " No less?" says he.
" Why sure, that's chape enough," says I. " Throth it
is," says he; " and I'm thinkin' it's *too* chape it is," says
he; " for if there wasn't somethin' the matther, it's not
for that you'd be selling the fine milch cow, as she is, to
all appearance?" " Indeed, thin," says I, " upon my
conscience she is a fine milch cow." " Maybe," says he,
" she's gone off her milk, in regard that she doesn't feed
well?" " Och, by this and that," says I, " in regard of
feedin' there's not the likes of her in Ireland; so make
your mind aisy, and if you like her for the money, you
may have her." " Why, indeed, I'm not in a hurry,"
says he, " and I'll wait till I see how they go in the fair."

" With all my heart," says I, purtendin' to be no ways
consarned, but in throth I began to be afeared that the
people was seein' somethin' unnath'ral about her, and
that we'd never get rid of her at all, at all. At last, we
kem to the fair, and a great sight o' people was in it—
throth you'd think the whole world was there, let alone
the standin's o' gingerbread and illigant ribbons, and
makin's o' beautiful gownds, and pitch-and-toss, and
merry-go-roun's, and tints with the best av drink in thim,
and the fiddles playin' up t' incourage the boys and girls;
but I never minded them at all, but detarmint to sell the

thievin' rogue of a cow afore I'd mind any divarshin in life, so an I dhriv her into the thick av the fair, whin all of a suddint, as I kem to the door av a tint, up sthruck the pipes to the tune av "Tattherin' Jack Welsh", and my jew'l, in a minit, the cow cock'd her ears, and was makin' a dart at the tint.

"Oh, murther!" says I, to the boys standin' by, "hould her," says I, "hould her—she ate one piper already, the vagabone, and, bad luck to her, she wants another now."

"Is it a cow for to ate a piper?" says one o' thim.

"Divil a word o' lie in it, for I seen his corps myself, and nothin' left but the two legs," says I; "and it's a folly to be sthrivin' to hide it, for I *see* she'll never lave it aff—as poor Paddy Grogan knows to his cost, Lord be marciful to him."

"Who's that takin' my name in vain?" says a voice in the crowd; and with that, shovin' the throng a one side, who the divil should I see but Paddy Grogan, to all appearance.

"Oh, hould him too," says I; "keep him av me, for it's not himself at all, but his ghost," says I; "for he was kilt last night, to my sartin knowledge, every inch av him, all to his legs."

Well, sir, with that Paddy—for it *was* Paddy himself, as it kem out afther—fell a laughin', and that you'd think his sides 'ud split; and whin he kem to himself, he ups and he tould uz how it was, as I tould you already; and the likes av the fun they made av me, was beyant tellin', for wrongfully misdoubtin' the poor cow, and layin' the blame of atin' a piper an her. So we all wint into the tint to have it explained, and by gor it took a full gallon o' sper'ts t' explain it; and we dhrank health and long life to Paddy and the cow, and Paddy played that day beyant

all tellin', and mony a one said the likes was never heerd
before or sence, even from Paddy himself—and av coorse
the poor slandered cow was dhruv home agin, and many
a quiet day she had wid uz afther that; and whin she
died, throth my father had sitch a regard for the poor
thing, that he had her skinned, and an illigant pair of
breeches made out iv her hide, and it's in the fam'ly to
this day; and isn't it mighty remarkable it is, what I'm
goin' to tell you now, but it's as thrue as I'm here, that
from that out, any one that has thim breeches an, the
minit a pair o' pipes sthrikes up, they can't rest, but
goes jiggin' and jiggin' in their sate, and never stops
as long as the pipes is playin'—and there, there is the
very breeches that's an me now, and a fine pair they are
this minit.

Mr. Higginbotham's Catastrophe

NATHANIEL HAWTHORNE

Nathaniel Hawthorne was born at Salem, Massachusetts, in 1804 and died in 1864. He came of an old New England family, and his Puritan heritage and upbringing were the dominating influences in his life and work. He held various posts in the customs service, and from 1853 till 1857 was United States consul at Liverpool. His best-known works are *The Tanglewood Tales*, and his novels *The Scarlet Letter* and *The House of the Seven Gables*. *Twice Told Tales* and *Mosses from an Old Manse* are collections of short stories—in them Hawthorne found a literary form peculiarly suited to the expression of his genius.

A young fellow, a tobacco pedlar by trade, was on his way from Morristown, where he had dealt largely with the Deacon of the Shaker settlement, to the village of Parker's Falls on Salmon River. He had a neat little cart, painted green, with a box of cigars depicted on each side panel, and an Indian chief holding a pipe and a golden tobacco stalk on the rear. The pedlar drove a smart little mare and was a young man of excellent character, keen at a bargain, but none the worse liked by the Yankees, who, as I have heard them say, would rather be shaved with a sharp razor than a dull one. Especially was he beloved by the pretty girls along the Connecticut, whose favour he used to court by presents of the best smoking tobacco in his stock, knowing well that the country lassies of New

England are generally great performers on pipes. Moreover, as will be seen in the course of my story, the pedlar was inquisitive and something of a tattler, always itching to hear the news and anxious to tell it again.

After an early breakfast at Morristown, the tobacco pedlar, whose name was Dominicus Pike, had travelled seven miles through a solitary piece of woods, without speaking a word to anybody but himself and his little grey mare. It being nearly seven o'clock, he was as eager to hold a morning gossip as a city shopkeeper to read the morning paper. An opportunity seemed at hand when, after lighting a cigar with a sunglass, he looked up and perceived a man coming over the brow of the hill, at the foot of which the pedlar had stopped his green cart. Dominicus watched him as he descended, and noticed that he carried a bundle over his shoulder on the end of a stick, and travelled with a weary yet determined pace. He did not look as if he had started in the freshness of the morning, but had footed it all night and meant to do the same all day.

" Good morning, mister," said Dominicus, when within speaking distance. " You go a pretty good jog. What's the latest news at Parker's Falls?"

The man pulled the broad brim of a grey hat over his eyes and answered, rather sullenly, that he did not come from Parker's Falls, which, as being the limit of his own day's journey, the pedlar had naturally mentioned in his inquiry.

"Well, then," rejoined Dominicus Pike, "let's have the latest news where you did come from. I'm not particular about Parker's Falls. Any place will answer."

Being thus importuned, the traveller—who was as ill-looking a fellow as one would desire to meet in a solitary piece of woods—appeared to hesitate a little, as if he were either searching his memory for news or weighing the expediency of telling it. At last, mounting on the step of the cart, he whispered in the ear of Dominicus, though he might have shouted aloud and no other mortal would have heard him.

" I do remember one little trifle of news," said he. " Old Mr. Higginbotham, of Kimballton, was murdered in his orchard at eight o'clock last night by an Irishman and a negro. They strung him up to the branch of a St. Michael's pear-tree, where nobody would find him till the morning."

As soon as this horrible intelligence was communicated, the stranger betook himself to his journey again, with more speed than ever, not even turning his head when Dominicus invited him to smoke a Spanish cigar and relate all the particulars. The pedlar whistled to his mare and went up the hill, pondering on the doleful fate of Mr. Higginbotham, whom he had known in the way of trade, having sold him many a bunch of long nines and a great deal of pigtail, lady's twist, and fig tobacco.

He was rather astonished at the rapidity with which the news had spread. Kimballton was nearly sixty miles distant in a straight line. The murder had been per- petrated only at eight o'clock the preceding night; yet Dominicus had heard of it at seven in the morning, when, in all probability, poor Mr. Higginbotham's own family had but just discovered his corpse, hanging on the St. Michael's pear-tree. The stranger on foot must have worn seven-league boots to travel at such a rate.

" Ill news flies fast, they say," thought Dominicus Pike; " but this beats railroads. The fellow ought to be hired to go express with the President's Message."

The difficulty was solved by supposing that the narrator had made a mistake of one day in the date of the occurrence; so that our friend did not hesitate to introduce the story at every tavern and country store along the road, expending a whole bunch of Spanish wrappers among at least twenty horrified audiences. He found himself invariably the first bearer of the intelligence, and was so pestered with questions that he could not avoid filling up the outline, till it became quite a respectable narrative.   He met with one piece of corroborative evidence. Mr. Higginbotham was a grader; and a former clerk of his, to whom Dominicus related the facts, testified that the old gentleman was accustomed to return home through the orchard about nightfall, with the money and valuable papers of the store in his pocket. The clerk manifested but little grief at Mr. Higginbotham's catastrophe, hinting, what the pedlar had discovered in his own dealings with him, that he was a crusty old fellow, as close as a vice. His property would descend to a pretty niece, who was now keeping school in Kimballton.

What with telling the news for the public good, and driving bargains for his own, Dominicus was so much delayed on the road that he chose to put up at a tavern about five miles short of Parker's Falls. After supper, lighting one of his prime cigars, he seated himself in the bar-room and went through the story of the murder, which had grown so fast that it took him half an hour to tell. There were as many as twenty people in the room, nineteen of whom received it all for gospel. The twentieth was an elderly farmer, who had arrived on horseback a short time before and was now seated in a corner smoking his pipe. When the story was concluded, he rose up very deliberately, brought his chair right in front of Dominicus, and stared him full in the face, puffing out the vilest tobacco smoke the pedlar had ever smelt.

" Will you make affidavit," demanded he, in the tone of a country justice taking an examination, " that old Squire Higginbotham of Kimballton was murdered in his orchard the night before last, and found hanging on his great pear-tree yesterday morning?"

" I tell the story as I heard it, mister," answered Dominicus, dropping his half-burnt cigar. " I don't say that I saw the thing done. So I can't take my oath that he was murdered exactly in that way."

" But I can take mine," said the farmer, " that if Squire Higginbotham was murdered the night before last, I drank a glass of bitters with his ghost this morning. Being a neighbour of mine, he called me into his store, as I was riding by, and treated me, and then asked me to do a little business for him on the road. He didn't seem to know any more about his own murder than I did."

" Why, then, it can't be a fact!" exclaimed Dominicus Pike.

" I guess he'd have mentioned it, if it was," said the old farmer; and he removed his chair back to the corner, leaving Dominicus quite down in the mouth.

Here was a sad resurrection of old Mr. Higginbotham! The pedlar had no heart to mingle in the conversation any more, but comforted himself with a glass of gin and water, and went to bed, where all night long he dreamed of hanging on the St. Michael's pear-tree. To avoid the old farmer (whom he so detested that his suspension would have pleased him better than Mr.

Higginbotham's), Dominicus rose in the grey of the morning, put the little mare into the green cart, and trotted swiftly away towards Parker's Falls. The fresh breeze, the dewy road, and the pleasant summer dawn revived his spirits and might have encouraged him to repeat the old story had there been anybody awake to hear it. But he met neither ox team, light wagon chaise, horseman, nor foot traveller, till, just as he crossed Salmon River, a man came trudging down to the bridge with a bundle over his shoulder, on the end of a stick.

"Good morning, mister," said the pedlar, reining in his mare. "If you come from Kimballton or that neighbourhood, maybe you can tell me the real fact about this affair of old Mr. Higginbotham. Was the old fellow actually murdered two or three nights ago, by an Irishman and a negro?"

Dominicus had spoken in too great a hurry to observe at first that the stranger himself had a deep tinge of negro blood. On hearing this sudden question, the Ethiopian appeared to change his skin, its yellow hue becoming a ghastly white, while, shaking and stammering, he thus replied:

"No! no! There was no coloured man! It was an Irishman that hanged him last night, at eight o'clock. I came away at seven! His folks can't have looked for him in the orchard yet."

Scarcely had the man spoken, when he interrupted himself, and though he seemed weary enough before, continued his journey at a pace which would have kept the pedlar's mare on a smart trot. Dominicus stared after him in great perplexity. If the murder had not been committed till Tuesday night, who was the prophet that had foretold it, in all its circumstances, on Tuesday

morning?   If Mr. Higginbotham's corpse was not yet
discovered by his own family, how came this man, at
above thirty miles' distance, to know that he was hanging
in the orchard, especially as he had left Kimballton
before the unfortunate man was hanged at all?   These
ambiguous circumstances, with the stranger's surprise
and terror, made Dominicus think of raising a hue and
cry after him, as an accomplice in the murder; since
a murder, it seemed, had really been perpetrated.

" But let the poor devil go," thought the pedlar.   " I
don't want his blood on my head; and hanging him
wouldn't unhang Mr. Higginbotham.   Unhang the old
gentleman! It's a sin, I know; but I should hate to have
him come to life a second time and give me the lie!"

With these meditations, Dominicus Pike drove into the
street of Parker's Falls, which, as everybody knows, is as
thriving a village as three cotton factories and a slitting
mill can make it.   The machinery was not in motion,
and but a few of the shop doors were unbarred, when he
alighted in the stable-yard of the tavern and made it his
business to order the mare four quarts of oats.

His second duty, of course, was to impart Mr. Higginbotham's catastrophe to the hostler.   He deemed it
advisable, however, not to be too positive as to the date
of the direful fact, and also to be uncertain whether it
were perpetrated by an Irishman and a negro, or by
the son of Erin alone.   Neither did he profess to relate
it on his own authority or that of any one person; he
mentioned it as a report generally diffused.

The story ran through the town like fire among girdled
trees, and became so much the universal talk that nobody
could tell whence it had originated.   Mr. Higginbotham
was as well known at Parker's Falls as any citizen of the

place, being part owner of the slitting mill and a considerable stockholder in the cotton factories. The inhabitants felt their own prosperity interested in his fate.

Such was the excitement that the Parker's Falls *Gazette* anticipated its regular day of publication, and came out with half a form of blank paper and a column of double pica emphasized with capitals and headed HORRID MURDER OF MR. HIGGINBOTHAM! Among other dreadful details, the printed account described the mark of the cord round the dead man's neck and stated the number of thousand dollars of which he had been robbed. There was much pathos also about the affliction of his niece, who had gone from one fainting fit to another, ever since her uncle was found hanging on the St. Michael's pear-tree with his pockets inside out. The village poet likewise commemorated the young lady's grief in seventeen stanzas of a ballad. The selectmen held a meeting and, in consideration of Mr. Higginbotham's claims on the town, determined to issue handbills, offering a reward of five hundred dollars for the apprehension of his murderers and the recovery of the stolen property.

Meanwhile the whole population of Parker's Falls, consisting of shopkeepers, mistresses of boarding-houses, factory girls, millmen, and schoolboys, rushed into the street and kept up such a terrible loquacity as more than compensated for the silence of the cotton machines, which refrained from their usual din out of respect to the deceased. Had Mr. Higginbotham cared about posthumous renown, his untimely ghost would have exulted in this tumult.

Our friend Dominicus, in his vanity of heart, forgot his intended precautions, and mounting on the town pump, announced himself as the bearer of the authentic intelligence which had caused so wonderful a sensation. He immediately became the great man of the moment, and had just begun a new edition of the narrative, with a voice like a field preacher, when the mail stage drove into the village street. It had travelled all night and must have shifted horses at Kimballton at three in the morning.

"Now we shall hear all the particulars," shouted the crowd.

The coach rumbled up to the piazza of the tavern, followed by a thousand people; for if any man had been minding his own business till then, he now left it at sixes and sevens, to hear the news. The pedlar, foremost in the race, discovered two passengers, both of whom had been startled from a comfortable nap to find themselves in the centre of a mob. Every man assailing them with separate questions, all propounded at once, the couple were struck speechless, though one was a lawyer and the other a young lady.

"Mr. Higginbotham! Mr. Higginbotham! Tell us the particulars about old Mr. Higginbotham!" bawled the mob. "What is the coroner's verdict? Are the murderers apprehended? Has Mr. Higginbotham's niece come out of her fainting fits? Mr. Higginbotham! Mr. Higginbotham!"

The coachman said not a word, except to swear awfully at the hostler for not bringing him a fresh team of horses. The lawyer inside had generally his wits about him even when asleep; the first thing he did, after learning the cause of the excitement, was to produce a large red pocket-book. Meanwhile Dominicus Pike, being an extremely polite young man, and also suspecting that a female tongue would tell the story as glibly as a lawyer's, had handed the lady out of the coach. She was a fine, smart girl, now wide awake and bright as a button, and had such a sweet, pretty mouth that Dominicus would almost as lief have heard a love tale from it as a tale of murder.

" Gentlemen and ladies," said the lawyer to the shop-keepers, the millmen, and the factory girls, " I can assure you that some unaccountable mistake, or, more probably, a wilful falsehood, maliciously contrived to injure Mr. Higginbotham's credit, has excited this singular uproar. We passed through Kimballton at three o'clock this morning, and most certainly should have been informed of the murder had any been perpetrated. But I have proof nearly as strong as Mr. Higginbotham's own oral testimony, in the negative. Here is a note relating to a suit of his in the Connecticut courts, which was delivered me from that gentleman himself. I find it dated at ten o'clock last evening."

So saying, the lawyer exhibited the date and signature of the note, which irrefragably proved, either that this perverse Mr. Higginbotham was alive when he wrote it, or—as some deemed the more probable case, of two doubtful ones—that he was so absorbed in worldly business as to continue to transact it even after his death. But unexpected evidence was forthcoming. The young lady, after listening to the pedlar's explanation, merely seized a moment to smooth her gown and put her curls in order, and then appeared at the tavern door, making a modest signal to be heard.

" Good people," said she, " I am Mr. Higginbotham's niece."

A wondering murmur passed through the crowd on beholding her so rosy and bright—that same unhappy niece, whom they had supposed, on the authority of the Parker's Falls *Gazette*, to be lying at death's door in a fainting fit. But some shrewd fellows had doubted, all along, whether a young lady would be quite so desperate at the hanging of a rich old uncle.

"You see," continued Miss Higginbotham, with a smile, "that this strange story is quite unfounded as to myself, and I believe I may affirm it to be equally so in regard to my dear Uncle Higginbotham. He has the kindness to give me a home in his house, though I contribute to my own support by teaching a school. I left Kimballton this morning to spend the vacation of commencement week with a friend, about five miles from Parker's Falls. My generous uncle, when he heard me on the stairs, called me to his bedside and gave me two dollars and fifty cents to pay my stage fare and another dollar for my extra expenses. He then laid his pocket-book under his pillow, shook hands with me, and advised me to take some biscuit in my bag, instead of breakfasting on the road. I feel confident, therefore, that I left my beloved relative alive, and trust that I shall find him so on my return."

The young lady curtsied at the close of her speech, which was so sensible and well worded, and delivered with such grace and propriety, that everybody thought her fit to be preceptress of the best academy in the State. But a stranger would have supposed that Mr. Higginbotham was an object of abhorrence at Parker's Falls, and that a thanksgiving had been proclaimed for his murder, so excessive was the wrath of the inhabitants on learning their mistake.

The millmen resolved to bestow public honours on Dominicus Pike, only hesitating whether to tar and feather

him, ride him on a rail, or refresh him with an ablution at
the town pump, on the top of which he had declared
himself the bearer of the news. The selectmen, by advice
of the lawyer, spoke of prosecuting him for a mis-
demeanour, in circulating unfounded reports, to the
great disturbance of the peace of the Commonwealth.
Nothing saved Dominicus, either from mob law or a
court of justice, but an eloquent appeal made by the
young lady in his behalf. Addressing a few words of
heartfelt gratitude to his benefactress, he mounted the
green cart and rode out of town, under a discharge of
artillery from the schoolboys, who found plenty of
ammunition in the neighbouring clay pits and mud-
holes. As he turned his head to exchange a farewell
glance with Mr. Higginbotham's niece, a ball, of the
consistency of hasty pudding, hit him slap in the mouth,
giving him a most grim aspect. His whole person was so
bespattered with the like filthy missiles that he had almost
a mind to ride back and supplicate for the threatened
ablution at the town pump; for, though not meant in
kindness, it would now have been a deed of charity.

However, the sun shone bright on poor Dominicus,
and the mud, an emblem of all stains of undeserved
opprobrium, was easily brushed off when dry. As he
was a funny rogue, his heart soon cheered up; nor could
he refrain from a hearty laugh at the uproar which his
story had excited. The handbills of the selectmen would
cause the commitment of all the vagabonds in the State.
The paragraph in the Parker's Falls *Gazette* would be
reprinted from Maine to Florida, and perhaps form an
item in the London newspapers; and many a miser
would tremble for his money-bags and life, on learning
the catastrophe of Mr. Higginbotham. The pedlar

meditated with much fervour on the charms of the young schoolmistress, and swore that Daniel Webster never spoke or looked so like an angel as Miss Higginbotham, while defending him from the wrathful populace at Parker's Falls.

Dominicus was now on the Kimballton turnpike, having all along determined to visit that place, though business had drawn him out of the most direct road from Morristown. As he approached the scene of the supposed murder, he continued to revolve the circumstances in his mind and was astonished at the aspect which the whole case assumed. Had nothing occurred to corroborate the story of the first traveller, it might now have been considered as a hoax; but the negro was evidently acquainted with either the report or the fact, and there was a mystery in his dismayed and guilty look on being abruptly questioned. When, to this singular combination of incidents, it was added that the rumour tallied exactly with Mr. Higginbotham's character and habits of life, and that he had an orchard and a St. Michael's pear-tree, near which he always passed at nightfall, the circumstantial evidence appeared so strong that Dominicus doubted whether the autograph produced by the lawyer, or even the niece's direct testimony, ought to be equivalent. Making cautious inquiries along the road, the pedlar further learned that Mr. Higginbotham had in his service an Irishman of doubtful character, whom he had hired without a recommendation, on the score of economy.

" May I be hanged myself," exclaimed Dominicus Pike aloud, on reaching the top of a lonely hill, " if I'll believe old Higginbotham is unhanged till I see him with my own eyes, and hear it from his own mouth! And as he's a real shaver, I'll have the minister or some other responsible man for an endorser."

It was growing dusk when he reached the toll-house on Kimballton turnpike, about a quarter of a mile from the village of this name. His little mare was fast bringing him up with a man on horseback, who trotted through the gate a few rods in advance of him, nodded to the toll-gatherer, and kept on towards the village. Dominicus was acquainted with the toll-man, and while making change, the usual remarks on the weather passed between them.

"I suppose," said the pedlar, throwing back his whip-lash, to bring it down like a feather on the mare's flank, "you have not seen anything of old Mr. Higginbotham within a day or two?"

"Yes," answered the toll-gatherer. "He passed the gate just before you drove up, and yonder he rides now, if you can see him through the dusk. He's been to Wood-field this afternoon attending a sheriff's sale there. The old man generally shakes hands and has a little chat with me; but to-night he nodded, as if to say, "Charge my toll," and jogged on; for wherever he goes, he must always be at home by eight o'clock."

"So they tell me," said Dominicus.

"I never saw a man look so yellow and thin as the squire does," continued the toll-gatherer. "Says I to myself, to-night, he's more like a ghost or an old mummy than good flesh and blood."

The pedlar strained his eyes through the twilight and could just discern the horseman, now far ahead on the village road. He seemed to recognize the rear of Mr. Higginbotham; but through the evening shadows and amid the dust from the horse's feet, the figure appeared dim and unsubstantial, as if the shape of the mysterious old man were faintly moulded of darkness and grey light.

Dominicus shivered. "Mr. Higginbotham has come back from the other world, by way of the Kimballton turnpike," thought he.

He shook the reins and rode forward, keeping about the same distance in the rear of the grey old shadow, till the latter was concealed by a bend of the road. On reaching this point, the pedlar no longer saw the man on horseback, but found himself at the head of the village street, not far from a number of stores and two taverns, clustered around the meeting-house steeple. On his left were a stone wall and a gate, the boundary of a wood lot, beyond which lay an orchard, farther still a mowing field, and last of all a house. These were the premises of Mr. Higginbotham, whose dwelling stood beside the old highway, but had been left in the background by the Kimballton turnpike. Dominicus knew the place; and the little mare stopped short by instinct, for he was not conscious of tightening the reins.

"For the soul of me, I cannot get by this gate!" said he, trembling. "I never shall be my own man again, till I see whether Mr. Higginbotham is hanging on the St. Michael's pear-tree!"

He leaped from the cart, gave the rein a turn around the gate-post, and ran along the green path of the wood lot as if Old Nick were chasing behind. Just then the village clock tolled eight, and as each deep stroke fell, Dominicus gave a fresh bound and flew faster than before, till, dim in the solitary centre of the orchard, he saw the fated pear-tree. One great branch stretched from the old contorted trunk across the path and threw the darkest shadow on that one spot. But something seemed to struggle beneath the branch!

The pedlar had never pretended to more courage than befits a man of peaceable occupation, nor could he account for his valour in this awful emergency. Certain it is, however, that he rushed forward, prostrated a sturdy Irishman with the butt end of his whip, and found— not indeed hanging on the St. Michael's pear-tree, but trembling beneath it, with a halter around his neck— the old, identical Mr. Higginbotham!

"Mr. Higginbotham," said Dominicus tremulously, "you're an honest man, and I'll take your word for it. Have you been hanged or not?"

If the riddle be not already guessed, a few words will explain the simple machinery by which this "coming event" was made to "cast its shadow before". Three men had plotted the robbery and murder of Mr. Higginbotham. Two of them, successively, lost courage and fled, each delaying the crime one night by their disappearance. The third was in the act of perpetration, when a champion, blindly obeying the call of Fate, like the heroes of old romance, appeared in the person of Dominicus Pike.

It only remains to say that Mr. Higginbotham took the pedlar into high favour, sanctioned his addresses to the pretty schoolmistress, and settled his whole property on their children, allowing themselves the interest. In due time, the old gentleman capped the climax of his favours by dying a Christian death, in bed, since which melancholy event Dominicus Pike has removed from Kimballton and established a large tobacco manufactory in my native village.

The Cask of Amontillado

EDGAR ALLAN POE

Edgar Allan Poe was born at Boston, Massachusetts, in 1809, and, being left an orphan at the age of three, was adopted by John Allan, a wealthy merchant. He received part of his education in England. After his return to America his eccentricities, dissipations, and frequent scrapes gradually estranged him from his patron, and in 1830 he found himself with no resources but his pen. During the next eighteen years he wrote stories and poems for various magazines in Baltimore and Philadelphia. He died in Baltimore in 1849. Poe was one of the earliest and most proficient writers of the modern short story. His best work deals with the weird, the grotesque, or the horrible, but, in the words of Andrew Lang, " his horrors are carefully designed and elaborated works, polished *ad unguem*; rather cold than frenzied,—witness *The Cask of Amontillado* ".

The thousand injuries of Fortunato I had borne as I best could; but when he ventured upon insult, I vowed revenge. You, who so well know the nature of my soul, will not suppose, however, that I gave utterance to a threat. *At length* I would be avenged; this was a point definitely settled—but the very definitiveness with which it was resolved, precluded the idea of risk. I must not only punish, but punish with impunity. A wrong is unredressed when retribution overtakes its redresser. It is equally unredressed when the avenger fails to make himself felt as such to him who has done the wrong.

It must be understood, that neither by word nor deed had I given Fortunato cause to doubt my good-will. I continued, as was my wont, to smile in his face, and he did not perceive that my smile *now* was at the thought of his immolation.

He had a weak point—this Fortunato—although in other regards he was a man to be respected and even feared. He prided himself on his connoisseurship in wine. Few Italians have the true virtuoso spirit. For the most part their enthusiasm is adapted to suit the time and opportunity—to practise imposture upon the British and Austrian millionaires. In painting and gemmary Fortunato, like his countrymen, was a quack —but in the matter of old wines he was sincere. In this respect I did not differ from him materially: I was skilful in the Italian vintages myself, and bought largely whenever I could.

It was about dusk, one evening during the supreme madness of the Carnival season, that I encountered my friend. He accosted me with excessive warmth, for he had been drinking much. The man wore motley. He had on a tight-fitting parti-striped dress, and his head was surmounted by the conical cap and bells. I was so pleased to see him, that I thought I should never have done wringing his hand.

I said to him, " My dear Fortunato, you are luckily met. How remarkably well you are looking to-day! But I have received a pipe of what passes for Amontillado, and I have my doubts."

" How?" said he; " Amontillado? A pipe? Impossible! And in the middle of the Carnival!"

" I have my doubts," I replied; " and I was silly enough to pay the full Amontillado price without consulting you in the matter. You were not to be found, and I was fearful of losing a bargain."

" Amontillado!"

" I have my doubts."

" Amontillado!"

" And I must satisfy them."

" Amontillado!"

" As you are engaged, I am on my way to Luchesi. If any one has a critical turn, it is he. He will tell me——"

" Luchesi cannot tell Amontillado from Sherry."

" And yet some fools will have it that his taste is a match for your own."

" Come, let us go."

" Whither?"

" To your vaults."

" My friend, no; I will not impose upon your good-nature. I perceive you have an engagement. Luchesi——"

" I have no engagement; come."

" My friend, no. It is not the engagement, but the severe cold with which I perceive you are afflicted. The vaults are insufferably damp. They are encrusted with nitre."

" Let us go nevertheless. The cold is merely nothing. Amontillado! You have been imposed upon. And as for Luchesi—he cannot distinguish Sherry from Amontillado."

Thus speaking, Fortunato possessed himself of my arm. Putting on a mask of black silk, and drawing a *roquelaire* closely about my person, I suffered him to hurry me to my palazzo.

There were no attendants at home; they had absconded to make merry in honour of the time. I had told them that I should not return until the morning, and had given them explicit orders not to stir from the house. These orders were sufficient, I well knew, to ensure their immediate disappearance, one and all, as soon as my back was turned.

I took from their sconces two flambeaux, and giving one to Fortunato, bowed him through several suites of rooms to the archway that led into the vaults. I passed down a long and winding staircase, requesting him to be cautious as he followed. We came at length to the foot of the descent, and stood together on the damp ground of the catacombs of the Montresors.

The gait of my friend was unsteady, and the bells upon his cap jingled as he strode.

"The pipe," said he.

"It is farther on," said I; "but observe the white webwork which gleams from these cavern walls."

He turned towards me, and looked into my eyes with two filmy orbs that distilled the rheum of in-toxication.

"Nitre?" he asked, at length.

"Nitre," I replied. "How long have you had that cough?"

"Ugh! ugh! ugh!—ugh! ugh! ugh!—ugh! ugh! ugh! —ugh! ugh! ugh!—ugh! ugh! ugh!"

My poor friend found it impossible to reply for many minutes.

"It is nothing," he said at last.

"Come," I said, with decision, "we will go back; your health is precious. You are rich, respected, admired, beloved; you are happy, as once I was. You are a man

to be missed. For me it is no matter. We will go back;
you will be ill, and I cannot be responsible. Besides,
there is Luchesi——"

" Enough," he said, " the cough is a mere nothing; it
will not kill me. I shall not die of a cough."

" True—true," I replied; " and, indeed, I had no
intention of alarming you unnecessarily—but you should
use all proper caution. A draught of this Médoc will
defend us from the damps."

Here I knocked off the neck of a bottle which I
drew from a long row of its fellows that lay upon the
mould.

" Drink," I said, presenting him the wine.

He raised it to his lips with a leer. He paused and
nodded to me familiarly, while his bells jingled.

" I drink," he said, " to the buried that repose around
us."

" And I to your long life."

He again took my arm, and we proceeded.

" These vaults," he said, " are extensive."

" The Montresors," I replied, " were a great and
numerous family."

" I forget your arms."

" A huge human foot d'or, in a field azure; the foot
crushes a serpent rampant whose fangs are embedded
in the heel."

" And the motto?"

" *Nemo me impune lacessit.*"

" Good!" he said.

The wine sparkled in his eyes and the bells jingled.
My own fancy grew warm with the Médoc. We had
passed through walls with piled bones, with casks and
puncheons intermingling, into the inmost recesses of

the catacombs. I paused again, and this time I made bold to seize Fortunato by an arm above the elbow.

"The nitre!" I said; "see, it increases. It hangs like moss upon the vaults. We are below the river's bed. The drops of moisture trickle among the bones. Come, we will go back ere it is too late. Your cough——"

"It is nothing," he said; "let us go on. But first, another draught of the Médoc."

I broke and reached him a flagon of De Grâve. He emptied it at a breath. His eyes flashed with a fierce light. He laughed and threw the bottle upwards with a gesticulation I did not understand.

I looked at him in surprise. He repeated the movement—a grotesque one.

"You do not comprehend?" he said.

"Not I," I replied.

"Then you are not of the brotherhood."

"How?"

"You are not of the masons."

"Yes, yes," I said; "yes, yes."

"You? Impossible! A mason?"

"A mason," I replied.

"A sign," he said.

"It is this," I answered, producing a trowel from beneath the folds of my *roquelaire*.

"You jest," he exclaimed, recoiling a few paces. "But let us proceed to the Amontillado."

"Be it so," I said, replacing the tool beneath the cloak, and again offering him my arm. He leaned upon it heavily. We continued our route in search of the Amontillado. We passed through a range of low arches, descended, passed on, and descending again, arrived at a deep crypt, in which the foulness of the air caused our flambeaux rather to glow than flame.

At the most remote end of the crypt there appeared another less spacious. Its walls had been lined with human remains, piled to the vault overhead, in the fashion of the great catacombs of Paris. Three sides of this interior crypt were still ornamented in this manner. From the fourth the bones had been thrown down, and lay promiscuously upon the earth, forming at one point a mound of some size. Within the wall thus exposed by the displacing of the bones, we perceived a still interior recess, in depth about four feet, in width three, in height six or seven. It seemed to have been constructed for no especial use within itself, but formed merely the interval between two of the colossal supports of the roof of the catacombs, and was backed by one of their circumscribing walls of solid granite.

It was in vain that Fortunato, uplifting his dull torch, endeavoured to pry into the depth of the recess. Its termination the feeble light did not enable us to see.

" Proceed," I said; " herein is the Amontillado. As for Luchesi——"

" He is an ignoramus," interrupted my friend, as he stepped unsteadily forward, while I followed immediately at his heels. In an instant he had reached the extremity of the niche, and finding his progress arrested by the rock, stood stupidly bewildered. A moment more and I had fettered him to the granite. In its surface were two iron staples, distant from each other about two feet, horizontally. From one of these depended a short chain, from the other a padlock. Throwing the links about his waist, it was but the work of a few seconds to secure it.

He was too much astounded to resist. Withdrawing the key, I stepped back from the recess.

" Pass your hand," I said, " over the wall; you cannot help feeling the nitre. Indeed it is *very* damp. Once more let me *implore* you to return. No? Then I must positively leave you. But I must first render you all the little attentions in my power."

" The Amontillado!" ejaculated my friend, not yet recovered from his astonishment.

" True," I replied, " the Amontillado."

As I said these words I busied myself among the pile of bones of which I have before spoken. Throwing them aside, I soon uncovered a quantity of building stone and mortar. With these materials, and with the aid of my trowel, I began vigorously to wall up the entrance of the niche.

I had scarcely laid the first tier of the masonry when I discovered that the intoxication of Fortunato had in a great measure worn off. The earliest indication I had of this was a low moaning cry from the depth of the recess. It was *not* the cry of a drunken man. There was then a long and obstinate silence. I laid the second tier, and the third, and the fourth; and then I heard the furious vibrations of the chain. The noise lasted for several minutes, during which, that I might hearken to it with the more satisfaction, I ceased my labours and sat down upon the bones. When at last the clanking subsided, I resumed the trowel, and finished without interruption the fifth, the sixth, and the seventh tier. The wall was now nearly upon a level with my breast. I again paused, and holding the flambeaux over the mason-work, threw a few feeble rays upon the figure within.

A succession of loud and shrill screams, bursting suddenly from the throat of the chained form, seemed to thrust me violently back. For a brief moment I hesitated—I trembled. Unsheathing my rapier, I began to grope with it about the recess; but the thought of an instant reassured me. I placed my hand upon the solid fabric of the catacombs, and felt satisfied. I re-approached the wall. I replied to the yells of him who clamoured. I re-echoed—I aided—I surpassed them in volume and in strength. I did this, and the clamourer grew still.

It was now midnight, and my task was drawing to a close. I had completed the eighth, the ninth, and the tenth tier. I had finished a portion of the last and the eleventh; there remained but a single stone to be fitted and plastered in. I struggled with its weight; I placed it partially in its destined position. But now there came from out the niche a low laugh that erected the hairs upon my head. It was succeeded by a sad voice, which I had difficulty in recognizing as that of the noble Fortunato. The voice said—

" Ha! ha! ha!—he! he!—a very good joke indeed —an excellent jest. We will have many a rich laugh about it at the palazzo—he! he! he!—over our wine— he! he! he!"

" The Amontillado!" I said.

" He! he! he!—he! he! he!—yes, the Amontillado. But is it not getting late? Will not they be awaiting us at the palazzo, the Lady Fortunato and the rest? Let us be gone."

" Yes," I said, " let us be gone."

" *For the love of God, Montresor!*"

" Yes," I said, " for the love of God!"

But to these words I hearkened in vain for a reply. I grew impatient. I called aloud—

" Fortunato!"

No answer. I called again—

" Fortunato!"

No answer still. I thrust a torch through the remaining aperture and let it fall within. There came forth in return only a jingling of the bells. My heart grew sick —on account of the dampness of the catacombs. I hastened to make an end of my labour. I forced the last stone into its position; I plastered it up. Against the new masonry I re-erected the old rampart of bones. For the half of a century no mortal has disturbed them. *In pace requiescat!*

The Squire's Story

ELIZABETH CLEGHORN GASKELL

Elizabeth Cleghorn Gaskell, whose maiden name was Steven-son, was born at Chelsea in 1810, and died in 1865. She was brought up by an aunt at Knutsford, Cheshire, the Cranford of her stories, and in 1832 she married William Gaskell, a Unitarian minister in Manchester. Her first book, *Mary Barton*, was published in 1848, and in 1857 her biography of Charlotte Brontë appeared. Mrs. Gaskell was at her best in delicate character sketches such as comprise *Cranford* (1853); indeed, all her stories, even those which have a definite moral or social purpose, are notable for acute observation and delinea-tion of character. *The Squire's Story*, which appeared first of all in Dickens's magazine, *Household Words*, is based on an episode in the local history of Knutsford.

In the year 1769, the little town of Barford was thrown into a state of great excitement by the intelligence that a gentleman (and " quite the gentleman," said the land-lord of the " George Inn ") had been looking at Mr. Clavering's old house. This house was neither in the town nor in the country. It stood on the outskirts of Barford, on the road-side leading to Derby. The last occupant had been a Mr. Clavering—a Northumberland gentleman of good family—who had come to live in Barford while he was but a younger son; but when some elder branches of the family died, he had returned to take possession of the family estate. The house of which I speak was called the White House, from its being covered with a greyish kind of stucco. It had a good garden to the back, and Mr. Clavering had built capital stables with what were then considered the latest improvements. The point of good stabling was expected to let the house, as it was in a hunting county; otherwise it had few recommendations. There were many bed-rooms; some entered through others, even to the number of five, leading one beyond the other; several sitting-rooms of the small and poky kind, wainscotted round with wood, and then painted a heavy slate colour; one good dining-room, and a drawing-room over it, both looking into the garden, with pleasant bow-windows.

Such was the accommodation offered by the White House. It did not seem to be very tempting to strangers, though the good people of Barford rather piqued them-selves on it as the largest house in the town, and as a house in which " townspeople " and " county people " had often met at Mr. Clavering's friendly dinners. To appreciate this circumstance of pleasant recollection, you should have lived some years in a little country town, surrounded by gentlemen's seats. You would then understand how a bow or a courtesy from a member of a county family elevates the individuals who receive it almost as much, in their own eyes, as the pair of blue garters fringed with silver did Mr. Bickerstaff's ward. They trip lightly on air for a whole day afterwards. Now Mr. Clavering was gone, where could town and county mingle?

I mention these things that you may have an idea of the desirability of the letting of the White House in the Barfordites' imagination; and to make the mixture thick and slab, you must add for yourselves the bustle, the mystery, and the importance which every little event either causes or assumes in a small town, and then perhaps it will be no wonder to you that twenty ragged little urchins accompanied the " gentleman " aforesaid to the door of the White House; and that, although he was above an hour inspecting it, under the auspices of Mr. Jones, the agent's clerk, thirty more had joined themselves on to the wondering crowd before his exit, and awaited such crumbs of intelligence as they could gather before they were threatened or whipped out of hearing distance. Presently, out came the " gentleman " and the lawyer's clerk. The latter was speaking as he followed the former over the threshold. The gentleman was tall, well-dressed, handsome; but there was a sinister cold look in his quick-glancing, light blue eye, which a keen observer might not have liked. There were no keen observers among the boys and ill-conditioned gaping girls. But they stood too near, inconveniently close; and the gentleman, lifting up his right hand, in which he carried a short riding-whip, dealt one or two sharp blows to the nearest, with a look of savage enjoyment on his face as they moved away whimpering and crying. An instant after, his expression of countenance had changed.

" Here!" said he, drawing out a handful of money, partly silver, partly copper, and throwing it into the midst of them. " Scramble for it! fight it out, my lads! come this afternoon, at three, to the ' George ', and I'll throw you out some more." So the boys hurrahed for him as he walked off with the agent's clerk. He chuckled to himself, as over a pleasant thought. " I'll have some fun with those lads," he said; " I'll teach 'em to come prowling and prying about me. I'll tell you what I'll do. I'll make the money so hot in the fire-shovel that it shall burn their fingers. You come and see the faces and the howling. I shall be very glad if you will dine with me at two, and by that time I may have made up my mind respecting the house."

Mr. Jones, the agent's clerk, agreed to come to the " George " at two, but somehow he had a distaste for his entertainer. Mr. Jones would not like to have said, even to himself, that a man with a purse full of money, who kept many horses, and spoke familiarly of noblemen—above all, who thought of taking the White House —could be anything but a gentleman; but still the uneasy wonder as to who this Mr. Robinson Higgins could be filled the clerk's mind long after Mr. Higgins, Mr. Higgins's servants, and Mr. Higgins's stud had taken possession of the White House.

The White House was re-stuccoed (this time of a pale yellow colour) and put into thorough repair by the accommodating and delighted landlord, while his tenant seemed inclined to spend any amount of money on internal decorations, which were showy and effective in their character, enough to make the White House a nine days' wonder to the good people of Barford. The slate-coloured paints became pink, and were picked out with gold; the old-fashioned banisters were replaced by newly gilt ones; but, above all, the stables were a sight to be seen. Since the days of the Roman Emperor never was there such provision made for the care, the comfort, and the health of horses. But every one said it was no wonder, when they were led through Barford, covered up to their eyes, but curving their arched and delicate necks, and prancing with short, high steps, in repressed eagerness. Only one groom came with them;

yet they required the care of three men. Mr. Higgins, however, preferred engaging two lads out of Barford; and Barford highly approved of his preference. Not only was it kind and thoughtful to give employment to the lounging lads themselves, but they were receiving such a training in Mr. Higgins's stables as might fit them for Doncaster or Newmarket. The district of Derbyshire in which Barford was situated was too close to Leicestershire not to support a hunt and a pack of hounds. The master of the hounds was a certain Sir Harry Manley, who was *aut* a huntsman *aut nullus*. He measured a man by the " length of his fork ", not by the expression of his countenance, or the shape of his head. But, as Sir Harry was wont to observe, there was such a thing as too long a fork, so his approbation was withheld until he had seen a man on horseback; and if his seat there was square and easy, his hand light, and his courage good, Sir Harry hailed him as a brother.

Mr. Higgins attended the first meet of the season, not as a subscriber, but as an amateur. The Barford huntsmen piqued themselves on their bold riding; and their knowledge of the country came by nature; yet this new strange man, whom nobody knew, was in at the death, sitting on his horse, both well breathed and calm, without a hair turned on the sleek skin of the latter, supremely addressing the old huntsman as he hacked off the tail of the fox; and he, the old man, who was testy even under Sir Harry's slightest rebuke, and flew out on any other member of the hunt that dared to utter a word against his sixty years' experience as stable-boy, groom, poacher, and what not—he, old Isaac Wormeley, was meekly listening to the wisdom of this stranger, only now and then giving one of his quick, up-turning, cunning glances, not unlike the sharp, o'er-canny looks of the poor deceased Reynard, round whom the hounds were howling, unadmonished by the short whip which was now tucked into Wormeley's well-worn pocket. When Sir Harry rode into the copse —full of dead brushwood and wet tangled grass—and was followed by the members of the hunt, as one by one they cantered past, Mr. Higgins took off his cap and bowed—half-deferentially, half-insolently—with a lurking smile in the corner of his eye at the discomfited looks of one or two of the laggards. "A famous run, sir," said Sir Harry. "The first time you have hunted in our country, but I hope we shall see you often."

"I hope to become a member of the hunt, sir," said Mr. Higgins.

"Most happy—proud, I am sure, to receive so daring a rider among us. You took the Cropper-gate, I fancy, while some of our friends here"—scowling at one or two cowards by way of finishing his speech. "Allow me to introduce myself—master of the hounds." He fumbled in his waistcoat pocket for the card on which his name was formally inscribed. "Some of our friends here are kind enough to come home with me to dinner; might I ask for the honour?"

"My name is Higgins," replied the stranger, bowing low. "I am only lately come to occupy the White House at Barford, and I have not as yet presented my letters of introduction."

"Hang it!" replied Sir Harry; "a man with a seat like yours, and that good brush in your hand, might ride up to any door in the county (I'm a Leicestershire man!), and be a welcome guest. Mr. Higgins, I shall be proud to become better acquainted with you over my dinner-table."

Mr. Higgins knew pretty well how to improve the acquaintance thus begun. He could sing a good song, tell a good story, and was well up in practical jokes; with plenty of that keen, worldly sense, which seems like an instinct in some men, and which in this case taught him on whom he might play off such jokes, with impunity from their resentment, and with a security of applause from the more boisterous, vehement, or prosperous. At the end of twelve months Mr. Robinson Higgins was, out-and-out, the most popular member of the Barford hunt; had beaten all the others by a couple of lengths, as his first patron, Sir Harry, observed one evening, when they were just leaving the dinner-table of an old hunting squire in the neighbourhood.

"Because, you know," said Squire Hearn, holding Sir Harry by the button—" I mean, you see, this young spark is looking sweet upon Catherine; and she's a good girl, and will have ten thousand pounds down, the day she's married, by her mother's will; and, excuse me, Sir Harry, but I should not like my girl to throw herself away."

Though Sir Harry had a long ride before him, and but the early and short light of a new moon to take it in, his kind heart was so much touched by Squire Hearn's trembling, tearful anxiety, that he stopped and turned back into the dining-room to say, with more asseverations than I care to give:

" My good squire, I may say, I know that man pretty well by this time; and a better fellow never existed. If I had twenty daughters he should have the pick of them."

Squire Hearn never thought of asking the grounds for his old friend's opinion of Mr. Higgins; it had been given with too much earnestness for any doubts to cross the old man's mind as to the possibility of its not being well-founded.   Mr. Hearn was not a doubter, or a thinker, or suspicious by nature; it was simply his love for Catherine, his only daughter, that prompted his anxiety in this case; and, after what Sir Harry had said, the old man could totter with an easy mind, though not with very steady legs, into the drawing-room, where his bonny, blushing daughter Catherine and Mr. Higgins stood close together on the hearth-rug; he whispering, she listening with downcast eyes.   She looked so happy, so like her dead mother had looked when the squire was a young man, that all his thought was how to please her most.   His son and heir was about to be married, and bring his wife to live with the squire; Barford and the White House were not distant an hour's ride; and, even as these thoughts passed through his mind, he asked Mr. Higgins if he could not stay all night—the young moon was already set—the roads would be dark— and Catherine looked up with a pretty anxiety, which, however, had not much doubt in it, for the answer.

With every encouragement of this kind from the old squire, it took everybody rather by surprise when, one morning, it was discovered that Miss Catherine Hearn was missing; and when, according to the usual fashion in such cases, a note was found, saying that she had eloped with " the man of her heart ", and gone to Gretna Green, no one could imagine why she could not quietly have stopped at home and been married in the parish church.   She had always been a romantic, sentimental girl; very pretty and very affectionate, and very much spoilt, and very much wanting in common sense. Her indulgent father was deeply hurt at this want of confidence in his never-varying affection; but when his son came, hot with indignation, from the baronet's (his future father-in-law's house, where every form of law and of ceremony was to accompany his own impending marriage), Squire Hearn pleaded the cause of the young couple with imploring cogency, and protested that it was a piece of spirit in his daughter, which he admired and was proud of. However, it ended with Mr. Nathaniel Hearn's declaring that he and his wife would have nothing to do with his sister and her husband. " Wait till you've seen him, Nat!" said the old squire, trembling with his distressful anticipations of family discord. " He's an excuse for any girl. Only ask Sir Harry's opinion of him." " Confound Sir Harry! So that a man sits his horse well Sir Harry cares nothing about anything else. Who is this man—this fellow? Where does he come from? What are his means? Who are his family?"

" He comes from the south—Surrey or Somersetshire, I forget which; and he pays his way well and liberally. There's not a tradesman in Barford but says he cares no more for money than for water; he spends like a prince, Nat. I don't know who his family are; but he seals with a coat of arms, which may tell you if you want to know; and he goes regularly to collect his rents from his estates in the south. Oh, Nat! if you would but be friendly, I should be as well pleased with Kitty's marriage as any father in the county."

Mr. Nathaniel Hearn gloomed and muttered an oath or two to himself. The poor old father was reaping the consequences of his weak indulgence to his two children. Mr. and Mrs. Nathaniel Hearn kept apart from Catherine

and her husband; and Squire Hearn durst never ask
them to Levison Hall, though it was his own house.
Indeed, he stole away as if he were a culprit whenever
he went to visit the White House; and if he passed a
night there he was fain to equivocate when he returned
home the next day; an equivocation which was well
interpreted by the surly, proud Nathaniel. But the
younger Mr. and Mrs. Hearn were the only people
who did not visit at the White House. Mr. and Mrs.
Higgins were decidedly more popular than their brother
and sister-in-law. She made a very pretty, sweet-
tempered hostess, and her education had not been such
as to make her intolerant of any want of refinement in
the associates who gathered round her husband. She
had gentle smiles for townspeople as well as county
people, and unconsciously played an admirable second
in her husband's project of making himself universally
popular.

But there is some one to make ill-natured remarks,
and draw ill-natured conclusions from very simple
premises, in every place; and in Barford this bird of
ill-omen was a Miss Pratt. She did not hunt—so Mr.
Higgins's admirable riding did not call out her admiration.
She did not drink—so the well-selected wines, so lavishly
dispensed among his guests, could never mollify Miss
Pratt. She could not bear comic songs, or buffo stories
—so, in that way, her approbation was impregnable.
And these three secrets of popularity constituted Mr.
Higgins's great charm. Miss Pratt sat and watched.
Her face looked immovably grave at the end of any of
Mr. Higgins's best stories; but there was a keen, needle-
like glance of her unwinking little eyes, which Mr.
Higgins felt rather than saw, and which made him

shiver, even on a hot day, when it fell upon him. Miss Pratt was a Dissenter, and to propitiate this female Mordecai, Mr. Higgins asked the Dissenting minister whose services she attended to dinner; kept himself and his company in good order; gave a handsome donation to the poor of the chapel. All in vain—Miss Pratt stirred not a muscle more of her face towards graciousness; and Mr. Higgins was conscious that, in spite of all his open efforts to captivate Mr. Davis, there was a secret influence on the other side, throwing in doubts and suspicions, and evil interpretations of all he said or did. Miss Pratt, the little, plain old maid, living on eighty pounds a year, was the thorn in the popular Mr. Higgins's side, although she had never spoken one uncivil word to him; indeed, on the contrary, had treated him with a stiff and elaborate civility.

The thorn—the grief to Mrs. Higgins was this. They had no children! Oh! how she would stand and envy the careless, busy motion of half a dozen children, and then, when observed, move on with a deep, deep sigh of yearning regret. But it was as well.

It was noticed that Mr. Higgins was remarkably careful of his health. He ate, drank, took exercise, rested by some secret rules of his own; occasionally bursting into an excess, it is true, but only on rare occasions— such as when he returned from visiting his estates in the south, and collecting his rents. That unusual exertion and fatigue—for there were no stage coaches within forty miles of Barford, and he, like most country gentlemen of that day, would have preferred riding if there had been—seemed to require some strange excess to compensate for it; and rumours went through the town that he shut himself up, and drank enormously for some days after his return. But no one was admitted to these orgies.

One day—they remembered it well afterwards—the hounds met not far from the town; and the fox was found in a part of the wild heath, which was beginning to be enclosed by a few of the more wealthy towns-people, who were desirous of building themselves houses rather more in the country than those they had hitherto lived in. Among these, the principal was a Mr. Dudgeon, the attorney of Barford, and the agent for all the county families about. The firm of Dudgeon had managed the leases, the marriage settlements, and the wills of the neighbourhood for generations. Mr. Dudgeon's father had the responsibility of collecting the land-owners' rents just as the present Mr. Dudgeon had at the time of which I speak; and as his son and his son's son have done since. Their business was an hereditary estate to them; and with something of the old feudal feeling was mixed a kind of proud humility at their position towards the squires whose family secrets they had mastered, and the mysteries of whose fortunes and estates were better known to the Messrs. Dudgeon than to themselves.

Mr. John Dudgeon had built himself a house on Wildbury Heath—a mere cottage, as he called it; but though only two storeys high it spread out far and wide, and work-people from Derby had been sent for on purpose to make the inside as complete as possible. The gardens, too, were exquisite in arrangement, if not very extensive; and not a flower was grown in them but of the rarest species. It must have been somewhat of a mortification to the owner of this dainty place when, on the day of which I speak, the fox, after a long race, during which he had described a circle of many miles, took refuge in the garden; but Mr. Dudgeon put a good face on the matter when a gentleman hunter, with the careless insolence of the squires of those days and that place, rode across the velvet lawn, and tapping at the window of the dining-room with his whip-handle, asked permission—no, that is not it!—rather, informed Mr. Dudgeon of their intention—to enter his garden in a body and have the fox unearthed. Mr. Dudgeon compelled himself to smile assent, with the grace of a masculine Griselda; and then he hastily gave orders to have all that the house afforded of provision set out for luncheon, guessing rightly enough that a six hours' run would give even homely fare an acceptable welcome. He bore without wincing the entrance of the dirty boots into his exquisitely clean rooms; he only felt grateful for the care with which Mr. Higgins strode about laboriously and noiselessly moving on the tip of his toes, as he reconnoitred the rooms with a curious eye.

" I'm going to build a house myself, Dudgeon; and, upon my word, I don't think I could take a better model than yours."

" Oh! my poor cottage would be too small to afford any hints for such a house as you would wish to build, Mr. Higgins," replied Mr. Dudgeon, gently rubbing his hands nevertheless at the compliment.

" Not at all! not at all! Let me see. You have dining-room, drawing-room—" he hesitated, and Mr. Dudgeon filled up the blank as he expected.

" Four sitting-rooms and the bed-rooms. But allow me to show you over the house. I confess I took some pains in arranging it, and, though far smaller than you would require, it may, nevertheless, afford you some hints."

So they left the eating gentlemen with their mouths and their plates quite full, and the scent of the fox over-powering that of the hasty rashers of ham, and they carefully inspected all the ground-floor rooms. Then Mr. Dudgeon said:

" If you are not tired, Mr. Higgins—it is rather my hobby, so you must pull me up if you are—we will go upstairs, and I will show you my sanctum."

Mr. Dudgeon's sanctum was the centre room over the porch, which formed a balcony, and which was carefully filled with choice flowers in pots. Inside there were all kinds of elegant contrivances for hiding the real strength of all the boxes and chests required by the particular nature of Mr. Dudgeon's business; for although his office was in Barford, he kept (as he informed Mr. Higgins) what was the most valuable here, as being safer than an office which was locked up and left every night. But, as Mr. Higgins reminded him with a sly poke in the side, when next they met, his own house was not over secure. A fortnight after the gentlemen of the Barford hunt lunched there, Mr. Dudgeon's strong-box—in his sanctum upstairs, with the mysterious spring-bolt to the window invented by himself, and the secret of which was only known to the inventor and a few of his most intimate friends, to whom he had proudly shown it—this strong-box, containing the collected Christmas rents of half a dozen landlords (there was then no bank nearer than Derby), was rifled, and the secretly rich Mr. Dudgeon had to stop his agent in his purchases of paintings by Flemish artists, because the money was required to make good the missing rents.

The Dogberries and Verges of those days were quite incapable of obtaining any clue to the robber or robbers;

and though one or two vagrants were taken up and brought before Mr. Dunover and Mr. Higgins, the magistrates who usually attended in the court-room at Barford, there was no evidence brought against them, and after a couple of nights' durance in the lock-ups they were set at liberty. But it became a standing joke with Mr. Higgins to ask Mr. Dudgeon, from time to time, whether he could recommend him a place of safety for his valuables, or if he had made any more inventions lately for securing houses from robbers.

About two years after this time—about seven years after Mr. Higgins had been married—one Tuesday evening, Mr. Davis was sitting reading the news in the coffee-room of the " George Inn ". He belonged to a club of gentlemen who met there occasionally to play at whist, to read what few newspapers and magazines were published in those days, to chat about the market at Derby, and prices all over the country. This Tuesday night it was a black frost, and few people were in the room. Mr. Davis was anxious to finish an article in the *Gentleman's Magazine*; indeed, he was making extracts from it, intending to answer it, and yet unable with his small income to purchase a copy. So he stayed late; it was past nine, and at ten o'clock the room was closed. But while he wrote, Mr. Higgins came in. He was pale and haggard with cold. Mr. Davis, who had had for some time sole possession of the fire, moved politely on one side, and handed to the new comer the sole London newspaper which the room afforded. Mr. Higgins accepted it, and made some remark on the intense coldness of the weather; but Mr. Davis was too full of his article and intended reply to fall into conversation readily. Mr. Higgins hitched his chair nearer to the fire, and put his feet on the fender, giving an audible shudder. He put the newspaper on one end of the table near him, and sat gazing into the red embers of the fire, crouching down over them as if his very marrow were chilled. At length he said:

" There is no account of the murder at Bath in that paper?" Mr. Davis, who had finished taking his notes, and was preparing to go, stopped short, and asked—

" Has there been a murder at Bath? No! I have not seen anything of it—who was murdered?"

" Oh! it was a shocking, terrible murder!" said Mr. Higgins, not raising his look from the fire, but gazing on with his eyes dilated till the whites were seen all round them. " A terrible, terrible murder! I wonder what will become of the murderer? I can fancy the red glowing centre of that fire—look and see how infinitely distant it seems, and how the distance magnifies it into something awful and unquenchable."

" My dear sir, you are feverish; how you shake and shiver!" said Mr. Davis, thinking, privately, that his companion had symptoms of fever, and that he was wandering in his mind.

" Oh, no!" said Mr. Higgins. " I am not feverish. It is the night which is so cold." And for a time he talked with Mr. Davis about the article in the *Gentleman's Magazine*, for he was rather a reader himself, and could take more interest in Mr. Davis's pursuits than most of the people at Barford. At length it drew near to ten, and Mr. Davis rose up to go home to his lodgings.

" No, Davis, don't go. I want you here. We will have a bottle of port together, and that will put Saunders into good humour. I want to tell you about this murder," he continued, dropping his voice, and speaking hoarse and low. " She was an old woman, and he killed her, sitting reading her Bible by her own fireside!" He looked at Mr. Davis with a strange, searching gaze, as if trying to find some sympathy in the horror which the idea presented to him.

" Whom do you mean, my dear sir? What is this murder you are so full of? No one has been murdered here."

" No, you fool! I tell you it was in Bath!" said Mr. Higgins, with sudden passion; and then, calming himself to most velvet-smoothness of manner, he laid his hand on Mr. Davis's knee, there, as they sat by the fire, and gently detaining him, began the narration of the crime he was so full of; but his voice and manner were constrained to a stony quietude: he never looked in Mr. Davis's face; once or twice, as Mr. Davis remembered afterwards, his grip tightened like a compressing vice.

" She lived in a small house in a quiet, old-fashioned street, she and her maid. People said she was a good old woman; but, for all that, she hoarded and hoarded, and never gave to the poor. Mr. Davis, it is wicked not to give to the poor—wicked—wicked, is it not? I always give to the poor, for once I read in the Bible that ' Charity covereth a multitude of sins '. The wicked old woman never gave, but hoarded her money, and saved and saved. Some one heard of it; I say she threw a temptation in his way, and God will punish her for it. And this man—or it might be a woman, who knows—and this person heard also that she went to church in the mornings and her maid in the afternoons; and so, while the maid was at church, and the street and the house quite still, and the darkness of a winter afternoon coming on, she was nodding over her Bible—and that, mark you! is a sin, and one that God will avenge sooner or later—

and a step came, in the dusk, up the stair, and that
person I told you of stood in the room. At first, he—
no! At first, it is supposed—for, you understand, all
this is mere guess-work—it is supposed that he asked
her civilly enough to give him her money, or to tell
him where it was; but the old miser defied him, and
would not ask for mercy and give up her keys, even
when he threatened her, but looked him in the face as
if he had been a baby. Oh, God! Mr. Davis, I once
dreamt, when I was a little, innocent boy, that I should
commit a crime like this, and I wakened up crying; and
my mother comforted me—that is the reason I tremble
so now—that and the cold, for it is very, very cold!"

"But did he murder the old lady?" asked Mr. Davis;
"I beg your pardon, sir, but I am interested by your
story."

"Yes, he cut her throat; and there she lies yet, in
her quiet little parlour, with her face upturned and al'
ghastly white, in the middle of a pool of blood. Mr.
Davis, this wine is no better than water; I must have
some brandy."

Mr. Davis was horror-struck by the story, which
seemed to have fascinated him as much as it had done
his companion.

"Have they got any clue to the murderer?" said he.
Mr. Higgins drank down half a tumbler of raw brandy
before he answered.

"No; no clue whatever. They will never be able to
discover him; and I should not wonder, Mr. Davis—
I should not wonder if he repented after all, and did
bitter penance for his crime; and if so—will there be
mercy for him at the last day?"

"God knows!" said Mr. Davis, with solemnity. "It

is an awful story," continued he, rousing himself; " I hardly like to leave this warm, light room and go out into the darkness after hearing it. But it must be done " —buttoning on his great coat—" I can only say I hope and trust they will find out the murderer and hang him. If you'll take my advice, Mr. Higgins, you'll have your bed warmed and drink a treacle posset just the last thing; and, if you'll allow me, I'll send you my answer to Philologus before it goes up to old Urban."

The next morning Mr. Davis went to call on Miss Pratt, who was not very well, and, by way of being agreeable and entertaining, he related to her all he had heard the night before about the murder at Bath; and really he made a very pretty connected story out of it, and interested Miss Pratt very much in the fate of the old lady—partly because of a similarity in their situations; for she also privately hoarded money, and had but one servant, and stopped at home alone on Sunday afternoons to allow her servant to go to church.

" And when did all this happen?" she asked.

" I don't know if Mr. Higgins named the day; and yet I think it must have been on this very last Sunday."

" And to-day is Wednesday. Ill news travels fast."

" Yes, Mr. Higgins thought it might have been in the London newspaper."

" That it could never be. Where did Mr. Higgins learn all about it?"

" I don't know; I did not ask. I think he only came home yesterday: he had been south to collect his rents, somebody said."

Miss Pratt grunted. She used to vent her dislike and suspicions of Mr. Higgins in a grunt whenever his name was mentioned.

"Well, I shan't see you for some days. Godfrey
Merton asked me to go and stay with him and his sister;
and I think it will do me good. Besides," added she,
"these winter evenings—and these murderers at large
in the country—I don't quite like living with only Peggy
to call to in case of need."

Miss Pratt went to stay with her cousin, Mr. Merton.
He was an active magistrate, and enjoyed his reputation
as such. One day he came in, having just received his
letters.

"Bad account of the morals of your little town here,
Jessy!" said he, touching one of his letters. "You've
either a murderer among you, or some friend of a
murderer. Here's a poor old lady at Bath had her throat
cut last Sunday week; and I've a letter from the Home
Office, asking to lend them ' my very efficient aid ', as
they are pleased to call it, towards finding out the culprit.
It seems he must have been thirsty, and of a comfortable
jolly turn; for before going to his horrid work he tapped
a barrel of ginger wine the old lady had set by to work;
and he wrapped the spigot round with a piece of a letter
taken out of his pocket, as may be supposed: and this
piece of a letter was found afterwards; there are only
these letters on the outside, ' ns, Esq., -arford, -egworth ',
which some one has ingeniously made out to mean
Barford, near Kegworth. On the other side, there is
some allusion to a race-horse, I conjecture, though the
name is singular enough—' Church-and-King-and-down-
with-the-Rump '."

Miss Pratt caught at this name immediately. It had
hurt her feelings as a Dissenter only a few months ago,
and she remembered it well.

"Mr. Nat Hearn has, or had (as I am speaking in

the witness-box, as it were, I must take care of my tenses), a horse with that ridiculous name."

" Mr. Nat Hearn," repeated Mr. Merton, making a note of the intelligence; then he recurred to his letter from the Home Office again.

" There is also a piece of a small key, broken in the futile attempt to open a desk—well, well. Nothing more of consequence. The letter is what we must rely upon."

" Mr. Davis said that Mr. Higgins told him—" Miss Pratt began.

" Higgins!" exclaimed Mr. Merton, " *ns*. Is it Higgins, the blustering fellow that ran away with Nat Hearn's sister?"

" Yes!" said Miss Pratt. " But though he has never been a favourite of mine—"

" *ns*," repeated Mr. Merton. " It is too horrible to think of; a member of the hunt—kind old Squire Hearn's son-in-law! Who else have you in Barford with names that end in *ns*?"

" There's Jackson, and Higginson, and Blenkinsop, and Davis, and Jones. Cousin! one thing strikes me—how did Mr. Higgins know all about it to tell Mr. Davis on Tuesday what had happened on Sunday afternoon?"

There is no need to add much more. Those curious in lives of the highwayman may find the name of Higgins as conspicuous among those annals as that of Claude Duval. Kate Hearn's husband collected his rents on the highway, like many another " gentleman " of the day; but, having been unlucky in one or two of his adventures, and hearing exaggerated accounts of the hoarded wealth of the old lady at Bath, he was led on from robbery to murder, and was hung for his crime at Derby, in 1775.

He had not been an unkind husband, and his poor wife took lodgings in Derby to be near him in his last moments—his awful last moments. Her old father went with her everywhere but into her husband's cell, and wrung her heart by constantly accusing himself of having promoted her marriage with a man of whom he knew so little. He abdicated his squireship in favour of his son Nathaniel. Nat was prosperous, and the helpless, silly father could be of no use to him; but to his widowed daughter the foolish, fond old man was all in all; her knight, her protector, her companion—her most faithful, loving companion. Only he ever declined assuming the office of her counsellor, shaking his head sadly, and saying,

" Ah! Kate, Kate! if I had had more wisdom to have advised thee better, thou need'st not have been an exile here in Brussels, shrinking from the sight of every English person as if they knew thy story."

I saw the White House not a month ago; it was to let, perhaps for the twentieth time since Mr. Higgins occupied it; but still the tradition goes in Barford that, once upon a time, a highwayman lived there, and amassed untold treasures, and that the ill-gotten wealth yet remains walled up in some unknown, concealed chamber, but in what part of the house no one knows.

Will any of you become tenants, and try to find out this mysterious closet? I can furnish the exact address to any applicant who wishes for it.

The Bagman's Story

CHARLES DICKENS

Charles Dickens was born at Landport, Portsmouth, in 1812, and died near Rochester in 1870. During his infancy his family removed to London, and the hardships of his early life there are reflected in his novel *David Copperfield*. He eventually became a journalist, and his first book, *Sketches by Boz*, appeared in 1836. In the same year *The Pickwick Papers* was published serially. This was the first of the long series of novels which firmly established his position as one of the greatest English novelists and humorists. Dickens did not find the short story an easy medium of expression, but the *Pickwick Papers* contains several excellently constructed short stories of which *The Bagman's Story* is one.

One winter's evening, about five o'clock, just as it began to grow dusk, a man in a gig might have been seen urging his tired horse along the road which leads across Marlborough Downs, in the direction of Bristol. I say he might have been seen, and I have no doubt he would have been, if anybody but a blind man had happened to pass that way; but the weather was so bad, and the night so cold and wet, that nothing was out but the water, and so the traveller jogged along in the middle of the road, lonesome and dreary enough. If any bagman of that day could have caught sight of the little neck-or-nothing sort of gig, with a clay-coloured body and red wheels, and the vixenish, ill-tempered, fast-going bay mare, that looked like a cross between a butcher's horse and a twopenny post-office pony, he would have known at once that this traveller could have been no other than Tom Smart, of the great house of Bilson and Slum, Cateaton Street, City. However, as there was no bagman to look on, nobody knew anything at all about the matter; and so Tom Smart and his clay-coloured gig with the red wheels, and the vixenish mare with the fast pace, went on together, keeping the secret among them, and nobody was a bit the wiser.

There are many pleasanter places, even in this dreary world, than Marlborough Downs when it blows hard; and if you throw in beside, a gloomy winter's evening, a miry and sloppy road, and a pelting fall of heavy rain, and try the effect, by way of experiment, in your own proper person, you will experience the full force of this observation.

The wind blew—not up the road or down it, though that's bad enough, but sheer across it, sending the rain slanting down like the lines they used to rule in the copybooks at school, to make the boys slope well. For a moment it would die away, and the traveller would begin to delude himself into the belief that, exhausted with its previous fury, it had quietly laid itself down to rest, when, whoo! he would hear it growling and whistling in the distance, and on it would come rushing over the hill-tops, and sweeping along the plain, gathering sound and strength as it drew nearer, until it dashed with a heavy gust against horse and man, driving the sharp rain into their ears, and its cold damp breath into their very bones; and past them it would scour, far, far away, with a stunning roar, as if in ridicule of their weakness, and triumphant in the consciousness of its own strength and power.

The bay mare splashed away, through the mud and water, with drooping ears; now and then tossing her head as if to express her disgust at this very ungentlemanly behaviour of the elements, but keeping a good pace notwithstanding, until a gust of wind, more furious than any that had yet assailed them, caused her to stop suddenly and plant her four feet firmly against the ground, to prevent her being blown over. It's a special mercy that she did this, for if she *had* been blown over, the vixenish mare was so light, and the gig was so light, and Tom Smart such a light weight into the bargain, that they must infallibly have all gone rolling over and over together, until they reached the confines of earth, or until the wind fell; and in either case the probability is, that neither the vixenish mare, nor the clay-coloured gig with the red wheels, nor Tom Smart, would ever have been fit for service again.

"Well, damn my straps and whiskers," says Tom Smart (Tom sometimes had an unpleasant knack of swearing)—"damn my straps and whiskers," says Tom, "if this ain't pleasant, blow me!"

You'll very likely ask me why, as Tom Smart had been pretty well blown already, he expressed this wish to be submitted to the same process again. I can't say—all I know is, that Tom Smart said so—or at least he always told my uncle he said so, and it's just the same thing.

"Blow me," says Tom Smart; and the mare neighed as if she were precisely of the same opinion.

"Cheer up, old girl," said Tom, patting the bay mare on the neck with the end of his whip. "It won't do pushing on, such a night as this; the first house we come to we'll put up at, so the faster you go the sooner it's over. Soho, old girl—gently—gently."

Whether the vixenish mare was sufficiently well acquainted with the tones of Tom's voice to comprehend his meaning, or whether she found it colder standing still than moving on, of course I can't say. But I can say that Tom had no sooner finished speaking, than she pricked up her ears, and started forward at a speed which made the clay-coloured gig rattle until you would have supposed every one of the red spokes were going to fly out on the turf of Marlborough Downs; and even Tom, whip as he was, couldn't stop or check her pace, until she drew up of her own accord, before a roadside inn on the right-hand side of the way, about half a quarter of a mile from the end of the Downs.

Tom cast a hasty glance at the upper part of the house as he threw the reins to the hostler, and stuck the whip in the box. It was a strange old place, built of a kind of shingle, inlaid, as it were, with cross-beams, with gabled-topped windows projecting completely over the pathway, and a low door with a dark porch, and a couple of steep steps leading down into the house, instead of the modern fashion of half a dozen shallow ones leading up to it. It was a comfortable-looking place though, for there was a strong, cheerful light in the bar window, which shed a bright ray across the road, and even lighted up the hedge on the other side; and there was a red flickering light in the opposite window, one moment but faintly discernible, and the next gleaming strongly through the drawn curtains, which intimated that a rousing fire was blazing within. Marking these little evidences with the eye of an experienced traveller, Tom dismounted with as much agility as his half-frozen limbs would permit, and entered the house.

In less than five minutes' time, Tom was ensconced in

the room opposite the bar—the very room where he had imagined the fire blazing—before a substantial, matter-of-fact, roaring fire, composed of something short of a bushel of coals, and wood enough to make half a dozen decent gooseberry bushes, piled half-way up the chimney, and roaring and crackling with a sound that of itself would have warmed the heart of any reasonable man. This was comfortable, but this was not all; for a smartly-dressed girl, with a bright eye and a neat ankle, was laying a very clean white cloth on the table; and as Tom sat with his slippered feet on the fender, and his back to the open door, he saw a charming prospect of the bar reflected in the glass over the chimney-piece, with delightful rows of green bottles and gold labels, together with jars of pickles and preserves, and cheeses and boiled hams, and rounds of beef, arranged on shelves in the most tempting and delicious array. Well, this was comfortable too; but even this was not all—for in the bar, seated at tea at the nicest possible little table, drawn close up before the brightest possible little fire, was a buxom widow of somewhere about eight-and-forty or thereabouts, with a face as comfortable as the bar, who was evidently the landlady of the house, and the supreme ruler over all these agreeable possessions. There was only one drawback to the beauty of the whole picture, and that was a tall man—a very tall man—in a brown coat and bright basket buttons, and black whiskers and wavy black hair, who was seated at tea with the widow, and who it required no great penetration to discover was in a fair way of per-suading her to be a widow no longer, but to confer upon him the privilege of sitting down in that bar, for and during the whole remainder of the term of his natural life.

Tom Smart was by no means of an irritable or envious disposition, but somehow or other the tall man with the brown coat and the bright basket buttons did rouse what little gall he had in his composition, and did make him feel extremely indignant, the more especially as he could now and then observe, from his seat before the glass, certain little affectionate familiarities passing between the tall man and the widow, which sufficiently denoted that the tall man was as high in favour as he was in size. Tom was fond of hot punch—I may venture to say he was *very* fond of hot punch—and after he had seen the vixenish mare well fed and well littered down, and had eaten every bit of the nice little hot dinner which the widow tossed up for him with her own hands, he just ordered a tumbler of it by way of experiment. Now, if there was one thing in the whole range of domestic art, which the widow could manufacture better than another, it was this identical article; and the first tumbler was adapted to Tom Smart's taste with such peculiar nicety, that he ordered a second with the least possible delay. Hot punch is a pleasant thing, gentlemen—an extremely pleasant thing under any circumstances—but in that snug old parlour, before the roaring fire, with the wind blowing outside till every timber in the old house creaked again, Tom Smart found it perfectly delightful. He ordered another tumbler, and then another—I am not quite certain whether he didn't order another after that—but the more he drank of the hot punch, the more he thought of the tall man.

"Confound his impudence!" said Tom to himself, "what business has he in that snug bar? Such an ugly villain too!" said Tom. "If the widow had any taste, she might surely pick up some better fellow than that." Here Tom's eye wandered from the glass on the chimney-piece to the glass on the table; and as he felt himself becoming gradually sentimental, he emptied the fourth tumbler of punch and ordered a fifth.

Tom Smart, gentlemen, had always been very much attached to the public line. It had long been his ambition to stand in a bar of his own, in a green coat, knee-cords, and tops. He had a great notion of taking the chair at convivial dinners, and he had often thought how well he could preside in a room of his own in the talking way, and what a capital example he could set to his customers in the drinking department. All these things passed rapidly through Tom's mind as he sat drinking the hot punch by the roaring fire, and he felt very justly and properly indignant that the tall man should be in a fair way of keeping such an excellent house, while he, Tom Smart, was as far off from it as ever. So, after deliberating over the two last tumblers, whether he hadn't a perfect right to pick a quarrel with the tall man for having contrived to get into the good graces of the buxom widow, Tom Smart at last arrived at the satisfactory conclusion that he was a very ill-used and persecuted individual, and had better go to bed.

Up a wide and ancient staircase the smart girl preceded Tom, shading the chamber candle with her hand, to protect it from the currents of air which in such a rambling old place might have found plenty of room to disport themselves in, without blowing the candle out, but which did blow it out nevertheless—thus affording Tom's enemies an opportunity of asserting that it was he, and not the wind, who extinguished the candle, and that while he pretended to be blowing it alight again, he was in fact kissing the girl. Be this as it may, another light was obtained, and Tom was conducted through a maze of rooms, and a labyrinth of passages, to the apartment which had been prepared for his reception, where the girl bade him good-night and left him alone.

It was a good large room with big closets, and a bed which might have served for a whole boarding-school, to say nothing of a couple of oaken presses that would have held the baggage of a small army; but what struck Tom's fancy most was a strange, grim-looking, high-backed chair, carved in the most fantastic manner, with a flowered damask cushion, and the round knobs at the bottom of the legs carefully tied up in red cloth, as if it had got the gout in its toes. Of any other queer chair, Tom would only have thought it *was* a queer chair, and there would have been an end of the matter; but there was something about this particular chair, and yet he couldn't tell what it was, so odd and so unlike any other piece of furniture he had ever seen, that it seemed to fascinate him. He sat down before the fire, and stared at the old chair for half an hour. —Damn the chair, it was such a strange old thing, he couldn't take his eyes off it.

" Well," said Tom, slowly undressing himself, and staring at the old chair all the while, which stood with a mysterious aspect by the bedside, " I never saw such a rum concern as that in my days. Very odd," said Tom, who had got rather sage with the hot punch—" very odd." Tom shook his head with an air of profound wisdom, and looked at the chair again. He couldn't make anything of it though, so he got into bed, covered himself up warm, and fell asleep.

In about half an hour, Tom woke up with a start, from a confused dream of tall men and tumblers of punch; and the first object that presented itself to his waking imagination was the queer chair.

"I won't look at it any more," said Tom to himself, and he squeezed his eyelids together, and tried to persuade himself he was going to sleep again. No use; nothing but queer chairs danced before his eyes, kicking up their legs, jumping over each other's backs, and playing all kinds of antics.

"I may as well see one real chair, as two or three complete sets of false ones," said Tom, bringing out his head from under the bedclothes. There it was, plainly discernible by the light of the fire, looking as provoking as ever.

Tom gazed at the chair; and, suddenly as he looked at it, a most extraordinary change seemed to come over it. The carving of the back gradually assumed the lineaments and expression of an old, shrivelled human face; the damask cushion became an antique, flapped waistcoat; the round knobs grew into a couple of feet, encased in red cloth slippers; and the whole chair looked like a very ugly old man, of the previous century, with his arms akimbo. Tom sat up in bed, and rubbed his eyes to dispel the illusion. No. The chair was an ugly old gentleman; and what was more, he was winking at Tom Smart.

Tom was naturally a headlong, careless sort of dog, and he had had five tumblers of hot punch into the bargain; so, although he was a little startled at first, he began to grow rather indignant when he saw the old gentleman winking and leering at him with such an impudent air. At length he resolved that he wouldn't stand it; and as the old face still kept winking away as fast as ever, Tom said, in a very angry tone—

"What the devil are you winking at me for?"

"Because I like it, Tom Smart," said the chair; or the old gentleman, whichever you like to call him. He stopped

winking though, when Tom spoke, and began grinning
like a superannuated monkey.

" How do you know my name, old nut-cracker face?"
inquired Tom Smart, rather staggered; though he pretended to carry it off so well.

" Come, come, Tom," said the old gentleman, " that's
not the way to address solid Spanish mahogany. Damme,
you couldn't treat me with less respect if I was veneered."
When the old gentleman said this, he looked so fierce that
Tom began to grow frightened.

" I didn't mean to treat you with any disrespect, sir,"
said Tom, in a much humbler tone than he had spoken
in at first.

" Well, well," said the old fellow, " perhaps not—
perhaps not. Tom——"

" Sir——"

" I know everything about you, Tom; everything.
You're very poor, Tom."

" I certainly am," said Tom Smart. " But how came
you to know that?"

" Never mind that," said the old gentleman; " you're
much too fond of punch, Tom."

Tom Smart was just on the point of protesting that
he hadn't tasted a drop since his last birthday, but
when his eye encountered that of the old gentleman
he looked so knowing that Tom blushed, and was silent.

" Tom," said the old gentleman, " the widow's a fine
woman—remarkably fine woman—eh, Tom?" Here the
old fellow screwed up his eyes, cocked up one of his
wasted little legs, and looked altogether so unpleasantly
amorous, that Tom was quite disgusted with the levity
of his behaviour—at his time of life, too!

" I am her guardian, Tom," said the old gentleman.

" Are you?" inquired Tom Smart.

" I knew her mother, Tom," said the old fellow; " and her grandmother. She was very fond of me— made me this waistcoat, Tom."

" Did she?" said Tom Smart.

" And these shoes," said the old fellow, lifting up one of the red cloth mufflers; " but don't mention it, Tom. I shouldn't like to have it known that she was so much attached to me. It might occasion some unpleasantness in the family." When the old rascal said this, he looked so extremely impertinent, that, as Tom Smart afterwards declared, he could have sat upon him without remorse.

" I have been a great favourite among the women in my time, Tom," said the profligate old debauchee; " hundreds of fine women have sat in my lap for hours together. What do you think of that, you dog, eh!" The old gentleman was proceeding to recount some other exploits of his youth, when he was seized with such a violent fit of creaking that he was unable to proceed.

" Just serves you right, old boy," thought Tom Smart; but he didn't say anything.

" Ah!" said the old fellow, " I am a good deal troubled with this now. I am getting old, Tom, and have lost nearly all my rails. I have had an operation performed, too—a small piece let into my back—and I found it a severe trial, Tom."

" I dare say you did, sir," said Tom Smart.

" However," said the old gentleman, " that's not the point. Tom! I want you to marry the widow."

" Me, sir!" said Tom.

" You," said the old gentleman.

" Bless your reverend locks," said Tom (he had a few scattered horse-hairs left)—" bless your reverend

locks, she wouldn't have me." And Tom sighed involuntarily, as he thought of the bar.

"Wouldn't she?" said the old gentleman firmly.

"No, no," said Tom; "there's somebody else in the
wind. A tall man—a confoundedly tall man—with black
whiskers."

"Tom," said the old gentleman; "she will never
have him."

"Won't she?" said Tom. "If you stood in the bar,
old gentleman, you'd tell another story."

"Pooh, pooh," said the old gentleman. "I know all
about that."

"About what?" said Tom.

"The kissing behind the door, and all that sort of
thing, Tom," said the old gentleman. And here he gave
another impudent look, which made Tom very wroth,
because as you all know, gentlemen, to hear an old
fellow, who ought to know better, talking about these
things, is very unpleasant—nothing more so.

"I know all about that, Tom," said the old gentleman. "I have seen it done very often in my time, Tom,
between more people than I should like to mention to
you; but it never came to anything after all."

"You must have seen some queer things," said Tom,
with an inquisitive look.

"You may say that, Tom," replied the old fellow, with
a very complicated wink. "I am the last of my family,
Tom," said the old gentleman, with a melancholy sigh.

"Was it a large one?" inquired Tom Smart.

"There were twelve of us, Tom," said the old gentleman; "fine, straight-backed, handsome fellows as you'd
wish to see. None of your modern abortions—all with
arms, and with a degree of polish, though I say it that

should not, which it would have done your heart good to behold."

" And what's become of the others, sir?" asked Tom Smart.

The old gentleman applied his elbow to his eye as he replied, " Gone, Tom, gone. We had hard service, Tom, and they hadn't all my constitution. They got rheumatic about the legs and arms, and went into kitchens and other hospitals; and one of 'em, with long service and hard usage, positively lost his senses—he got so crazy that he was obliged to be burnt. Shocking thing that, Tom."

" Dreadful!" said Tom Smart.

The old fellow paused for a few minutes, apparently struggling with his feelings of emotion, and then said—

" However, Tom, I am wandering from the point. This tall man, Tom, is a rascally adventurer. The moment he married the widow, he would sell off all the furniture, and run away. What would be the consequence? She would be deserted and reduced to ruin, and I should catch my death of cold in some broker's shop."

" Yes, but——"

" Don't interrupt me," said the old gentleman. " Of you, Tom, I entertain a very different opinion; for I well know that if you once settled yourself in a public-house, you would never leave it, as long as there was anything to drink within its walls."

" I am very much obliged to you for your good opinion, sir," said Tom Smart.

" Therefore," resumed the old gentleman, in a dicta-torial tone, " you shall have her, and he shall not."

" What is to prevent it?" said Tom Smart eagerly.

" This disclosure," replied the old gentleman; " he is already married."

" How can I prove it?" said Tom, starting half out of bed.

The old gentleman untucked his arm from his side, and having pointed to one of the oaken presses, immediately replaced it, in its old position.

" He little thinks," said the old gentleman, " that in the right-hand pocket of a pair of trousers in that press, he has left a letter, entreating him to return to his disconsolate wife, with six—mark me, Tom—six babies, and all of them small ones."

As the old gentleman solemnly uttered these words, his features grew less and less distinct, and his figure more shadowy. A film came over Tom Smart's eyes. The old man seemed gradually blending into the chair, the damask waistcoat to resolve into a cushion, the red slippers to shrink into little red cloth bags. The light faded gently away, and Tom Smart fell back on his pillow, and dropped asleep.

Morning aroused Tom from the lethargic slumber into which he had fallen on the disappearance of the old man. He sat up in bed, and for some minutes vainly endeavoured to recall the events of the preceding night. Suddenly they rushed upon him. He looked at the chair; it was a fantastic and grim-looking piece of furniture, certainly, but it must have been a remarkably ingenious and lively imagination that could have discovered any resemblance between it and an old man.

" How are you, old boy?" said Tom. He was bolder in the daylight—most men are.

The chair remained motionless, and spoke not a word.

" Miserable morning," said Tom. No. The chair would not be drawn into conversation.

" Which press did you point to?—you can tell me that,"

said Tom. Devil a word, gentlemen, the chair would say.

"It's not much trouble to open it, anyhow," said Tom, getting out of bed very deliberately. He walked up to one of the presses. The key was in the lock; he turned it, and opened the door. There *was* a pair of trousers there. He put his hand into the pocket, and drew forth the identical letter the old gentleman had described!

"Queer sort of thing, this," said Tom Smart, looking first at the chair and then at the press, and then at the letter, and then at the chair again. "Very queer," said Tom. But, as there was nothing in either, to lessen the queerness, he thought he might as well dress himself, and settle the tall man's business at once—just to put him out of his misery.

Tom surveyed the rooms he passed through, on his way downstairs, with the scrutinizing eye of a landlord; thinking it not impossible, that before long, they and their contents would be his property. The tall man was standing in the snug little bar, with his hands behind him, quite at home. He grinned vacantly at Tom. A casual observer might have supposed he did it, only to show his white teeth; but Tom Smart thought that a consciousness of triumph was passing through the place where the tall man's mind would have been, if he had had any. Tom laughed in his face; and summoned the landlady.

"Good-morning, ma'am," said Tom Smart, closing the door of the little parlour as the widow entered.

"Good-morning, sir," said the widow. "What will you take for breakfast, sir?"

Tom was thinking how he should open the case, so he made no answer.

" There's a very nice ham," said the widow, " and a beautiful cold larded fowl. Shall I send 'em in, sir?"

These words roused Tom from his reflections. His admiration of the widow increased as she spoke. Thoughtful creature! Comfortable provider!

" Who is that gentleman in the bar, ma'am?" inquired Tom.

" His name is Jinkins, sir," said the widow, slightly blushing.

" He's a tall man," said Tom.

" He is a very fine man, sir," replied the widow, " and a very nice gentleman."

" Ah!" said Tom.

" Is there anything more you want, sir?" inquired the widow, rather puzzled by Tom's manner.

" Why, yes," said Tom. " My dear ma'am, will you have the kindness to sit down for one moment?"

The widow looked much amazed, but she sat down, and Tom sat down too, close beside her. I don't know how it happened, gentlemen—indeed my uncle used to tell me that Tom Smart said *he* didn't know how it happened either—but somehow or other the palm of Tom's hand fell upon the back of the widow's hand, and remained there while he spoke.

" My dear ma'am," said Tom Smart—he had always a great notion of committing the amiable—" my dear ma'am, you deserve a very excellent husband—you do indeed."

" Lor, sir!" said the widow—as well she might; Tom's mode of commencing the conversation being rather unusual, not to say startling; the fact of his never having set eyes upon her before the previous night being taken into consideration. " Lor, sir!"

" I scorn to flatter, my dear ma'am," said Tom Smart. " You deserve a very admirable husband, and whoever he is, he'll be a very lucky man." As Tom said this, his eye involuntarily wandered from the widow's face to the comforts around him.

The widow looked more puzzled than ever, and made an effort to rise. Tom gently pressed her hand, as if to detain her, and she kept her seat. Widows, gentlemen, are not usually timorous, as my uncle used to say.

" I am sure I am very much obliged to you, sir, for your good opinion," said the buxom landlady, half laughing; " and if ever I marry again——"

" *If*," said Tom Smart, looking very shrewdly out of the right-hand corner of his left eye. " *If*."

" Well," said the widow, laughing outright this time, " *when* I do, I hope I shall have as good a husband as you describe."

" Jinkins, to wit," said Tom.

" Lor, sir!" exclaimed the widow.

" Oh, don't tell me," said Tom, " I know him."

" I am sure nobody who knows him, knows anything bad of him," said the widow, bridling up at the mysterious air with which Tom had spoken.

" Hem!" said Tom Smart.

The widow began to think it was high time to cry, so she took out her handkerchief, and inquired whether Tom wished to insult her, whether he thought it like a gentleman to take away the character of another gentleman behind his back, why, if he had got anything to say, he didn't say it to the man, like a man, instead of terrifying a poor weak woman in that way; and so forth.

" I'll say it to him fast enough," said Tom, " only I want you to hear it first."

"What is it?" inquired the widow, looking intently in Tom's countenance.

"I'll astonish you," said Tom, putting his hand in his pocket.

"If it is, that he wants money," said the widow, "I know that already, and you needn't trouble yourself."

"Pooh, nonsense, that's nothing," said Tom Smart, "*I* want money. 'Tain't that."

"Oh, dear, what can it be?" exclaimed the poor widow.

"Don't be frightened," said Tom Smart. He slowly drew forth the letter, and unfolded it. "You won't scream?" said Tom doubtfully.

"No, no," replied the widow; "let me see it."

"You won't go fainting away, or any of that nonsense?" said Tom.

"No, no," returned the widow hastily.

"And don't run out, and blow him up," said Tom; "because I'll do all that for you. You had better not exert yourself."

"Well, well," said the widow, "let me see it."

"I will," replied Tom Smart; and, with these words, he placed the letter in the widow's hand.

Gentlemen, I have heard my uncle say that Tom Smart said the widow's lamentations when she heard the disclosure would have pierced a heart of stone. Tom was certainly very tender-hearted, but they pierced his, to the very core. The widow rocked herself to and fro, and wrung her hands.

"Oh, the deception and villainy of the man!" said the widow.

"Frightful, my dear ma'am; but compose yourself," said Tom Smart.

" Oh, I can't compose myself," shrieked the widow. " I shall never find anyone else I can love so much!"

" Oh, yes you will, my dear soul," said Tom Smart, letting fall a shower of the largest-sized tears, in pity for the widow's misfortunes. Tom Smart, in the energy of his compassion, had put his arm round the widow's waist; and the widow, in a passion of grief, had clasped Tom's hand. She looked up in Tom's face, and smiled through her tears. Tom looked down in hers, and smiled through his.

I never could find out, gentlemen, whether Tom did or did not kiss the widow at that particular moment. He used to tell my uncle he didn't, but *I* have my doubts about it. Between ourselves, gentlemen, I rather think he did.

At all events, Tom kicked the very tall man out at the front door half an hour after, and married the widow a month after. And he used to drive about the country, with the clay-coloured gig with the red wheels, and the vixenish mare with the fast pace, till he gave up business many years afterwards, and went to France with his wife; and then the old house was pulled down.

Malachi's Cove

ANTHONY TROLLOPE

Anthony Trollope was born in London in 1815 and died in 1882. In 1834 he obtained a clerkship in the General Post Office and remained in the postal service till his retirement in 1867. His duties took him all over the British Isles, as well as to Egypt, the West Indies, and the United States of America, and he thus obtained a wealth of material for novels, of which he wrote over sixty, books of travel, and short stories. His most famous novels are *The Three Clerks* (1858), *Orley Farm* (1862), and the Barsetshire novels, *The Warden* (1855), *Barchester Towers* (1857), *Doctor Thorne* (1858), *Framley Parsonage* (1861), *The Small House at Allington* (1864), and *The Last Chronicle of Barset* (1867). His novels present a faithful and realistic picture of the society of his time. Trollope contributed many short stories to various magazines.

On the northern coast of Cornwall, between Tintagel and Bossiney, down on the very margin of the sea, there lived not long since an old man who got his living by saving seaweed from the waves, and selling it for manure. The cliffs there are bold and fine, and the sea beats in upon them from the north with a grand violence. I doubt whether it be not the finest morsel of cliff scenery in England, though it is beaten by many portions of the west coast of Ireland, and perhaps also by spots in Wales and Scotland. Cliffs should be nearly precipitous, they should be broken in their outlines, and should barely admit here and there of an insecure passage from their summit to the sand at their feet. The sea should come, if not up to them, at least very near to them, and then, above all things, the water below them should be blue, and not of that dead leaden colour which is so familiar to us in England. At Tintagel all these requisites are there, except that bright blue colour which is so lovely. But the cliffs themselves are bold and well broken, and the margin of sand at high water is very narrow,—so narrow that at spring-tides there is barely a footing there.

Close upon this margin was the cottage or hovel of Malachi Trenglos, the old man of whom I have spoken. But Malachi, or old Glos, as he was commonly called by the people around him, had not built his house absolutely upon the sand. There was a fissure in the rock so great that at the top it formed a narrow ravine, and so complete from the summit to the base that it afforded an opening for a steep and rugged track from the top of the rock to the bottom. This fissure was so wide at the bottom that it had afforded space for Trenglos to fix his habitation on a foundation of rock, and here he had lived for many years. It was told of him that in the early days of his trade he had always carried the weed in a basket on his back to the top, but latterly he had been possessed of a donkey which had been trained to go up and down the steep track with a single pannier over his loins, for the rocks would not admit of panniers hanging by his side; and for this assistant he had built a shed adjoining his own, and almost as large as that in which he himself resided.

But, as years went on, old Glos procured other assistance than that of the donkey, or, as I should rather say, Providence supplied him with other help; and, indeed,

had it not been so, the old man must have given up his
cabin and his independence and gone into the workhouse
at Camelford. For rheumatism had afflicted him, old
age had bowed him till he was nearly double, and by
degrees he became unable to attend the donkey on its
upward passage to the world above, or even to assist in
rescuing the coveted weed from the waves.

At the time to which our story refers Trenglos had
not been up the cliff for twelve months, and for the last
six months he had done nothing towards the furtherance
of his trade, except to take the money and keep it, if any
of it was kept, and occasionally to shake down a bundle
of fodder for the donkey. The real work of the business
was done altogether by Mahala Trenglos, his granddaughter.

Mally Trenglos was known to all the farmers round
the coast, and to all the small tradespeople in Camelford.
She was a wild-looking, almost unearthly creature, with
wild-flowing, black, uncombed hair, small in stature,
with small hands and bright black eyes; but people said
that she was very strong, and the children around declared that she worked day and night, and knew nothing
of fatigue. As to her age there were many doubts. Some
said she was ten, and others five-and-twenty, but the
reader may be allowed to know that at this time she had
in truth passed her twentieth birthday. The old people
spoke well of Mally, because she was so good to her
grandfather; and it was said of her that though she
carried to him a little gin and tobacco almost daily, she
bought nothing for herself;—and as to the gin, no one
who looked at her would accuse her of meddling with
that. But she had no friends, and but few acquaintances
among people of her own age. They said that she was

fierce and ill-natured, that she had not a good word for
any one, and that she was, complete at all points, a
thorough little vixen. The young men did not care for
her; for, as regarded dress, all days were alike with her.
She never made herself smart on Sundays. She was
generally without stockings, and seemed to care not at
all to exercise any of those feminine attractions which
might have been hers had she studied to attain them.
All days were the same to her in regard to dress; and,
indeed, till lately, all days had, I fear, been the same to
her in other respects. Old Malachi had never been seen
inside a place of worship since he had taken to live under
the cliff.

But within the last two years Mally had submitted
herself to the teaching of the clergyman at Tintagel, and
had appeared at church on Sundays, if not absolutely
with punctuality, at any rate so often that no one who
knew the peculiarity of her residence was disposed to
quarrel with her on that subject. But she made no difference in her dress on these occasions. She took her
place on a low stone seat just inside the church door,
clothed as usual in her thick red serge petticoat and loose
brown serge jacket, such being the apparel which she had
found to be best adapted for her hard and perilous work
among the waters. She had pleaded to the clergyman
when he attacked her on the subject of church attendance
with vigour that she had got no church-going clothes.
He had explained to her that she would be received there
without distinction to her clothing. Mally had taken him
at his word, and had gone, with a courage which certainly deserved admiration, though I doubt whether there
was not mingled with it an obstinacy which was less
admirable.

For people said that old Glos was rich, and that Mally might have proper clothes if she chose to buy them. Mr. Polwarth, the clergyman, who, as the old man could not come to him, went down the rocks to the old man, did make some hint on the matter in Mally's absence. But old Glos, who had been patient with him on other matters, turned upon him so angrily when he made an allusion to money, that Mr. Polwarth found himself obliged to give that matter up, and Mally continued to sit upon the stone bench in her short serge petticoat, with her long hair streaming down her face. She did so far sacrifice to decency as on such occasions to tie up her back hair with an old shoe-string. So tied it would remain through the Monday and Tuesday, but by Wednesday afternoon Mally's hair had generally managed to escape.

As to Mally's indefatigable industry there could be no manner of doubt, for the quantity of seaweed which she and the donkey amassed between them was very surprising. Old Glos, it was declared, had never collected half what Mally gathered together; but then the article was becoming cheaper, and it was necessary that the exertion should be greater. So Mally and the donkey toiled and toiled, and the seaweed came up in heaps which surprised those who looked at her little hands and light form. Was there not some one who helped her at nights, some fairy, or demon, or the like? Mally was so snappish in her answers to people that she had no right to be surprised if ill-natured things were said of her.

No one ever heard Mally Trenglos complain of her work, but about this time she was heard to make great and loud complaints of the treatment she received from some of her neighbours. It was known that she went with her plaints to Mr. Polwarth; and when he could not help her, or did not give her such instant help as she needed, she went—ah, so foolishly! to the office of a certain attorney at Camelford, who was not likely to prove himself a better friend than Mr. Polwarth.

Now the nature of her injury was as follows. The place in which she collected her seaweed was a little cove; the people had come to call it Malachi's Cove from the name of the old man who lived there;—which was so formed, that the margin of the sea therein could only be reached by the passage from the top down to Trenglos's hut. The breadth of the cove when the sea was out might perhaps be two hundred yards, and on each side the rocks ran out in such a way that both from north and south the domain of Trenglos was guarded from intruders. And this locality had been well chosen for its intended purpose.

There was a rush of the sea into the cove, which carried there large, drifting masses of seaweed, leaving them among the rocks when the tide was out. During the equinoctial winds of the spring and autumn the supply would never fail; and even when the sea was calm, the long, soft, salt-bedewed, trailing masses of the weed could be gathered there when they could not be found elsewhere for miles along the coast. The task of getting the weed from the breakers was often difficult and dangerous,—so difficult that much of it was left to be carried away by the next incoming tide.

Mally doubtless did not gather half the crop that was there at her feet. What was taken by the returning waves she did not regret; but when interlopers came upon her cove, and gathered her wealth,—her grandfather's wealth, beneath her eyes, then her heart was broken. It was this interloping, this intrusion, that drove poor Mally to the

Camelford attorney. But, alas, though the Camelford attorney took Mally's money, he could do nothing for her, and her heart was broken!

She had an idea, in which no doubt her grandfather shared, that the path to the cove was, at any rate, their property. When she was told that the cove, and sea running into the cove, were not the freeholds of her grandfather, she understood that the statement might be true. But what then as to the use of the path? Who had made the path what it was? Had she not painfully, wearily, with exceeding toil, carried up bits of rock with her own little hands, that her grandfather's donkey might have footing for his feet? Had she not scraped together crumbs of earth along the face of the cliff that she might make easier to the animal the track of that rugged way? And now, when she saw big farmers' lads coming down with other donkeys,—and, indeed, there was one who came with a pony; no boy, but a young man, old enough to know better than rob a poor old man and a young girl,— she reviled the whole human race, and swore that the Camelford attorney was a fool.

Any attempt to explain to her that there was still weed enough for her was worse than useless. Was it not all hers and his, or, at any rate, was not the sole way to it his and hers? And was not her trade stopped and impeded? Had she not been forced to back her laden donkey down, twenty yards she said, but it had, in truth, been five, because Farmer Gunliffe's son had been in the way with his thieving pony? Farmer Gunliffe had wanted to buy her weed at his own price, and because she had refused he had set on his thieving son to destroy her in this wicked way.

" I'll hamstring the beast the next time as he's down

here!" said Mally to old Glos, while the angry fire literally streamed from her eyes.

Farmer Gunliffe's small homestead—he held about fifty acres of land—was close by the village of Tintagel, and not a mile from the cliff. The sea-wrack, as they call it, was pretty well the only manure within his reach, and no doubt he thought it hard that he should be kept from using it by Mally Trenglos and her obstinacy.

"There's heaps of other coves, Barty," said Mally to Barty Gunliffe, the farmer's son.

"But none so nigh, Mally, nor yet none that fills 'emselves as this place."

Then he explained to her that he would not take the weed that came up close to hand. He was bigger than she was, and stronger, and would get it from the outer rocks, with which she never meddled. Then, with scorn in her eye, she swore that she could get it where he durst not venture, and repeated her threat of hamstringing the pony. Barty laughed at her wrath, jeered her because of her wild hair, and called her a mermaid.

"I'll mermaid you!" she cried. "Mermaid, indeed! I wouldn't be a man to come and rob a poor girl and an old cripple. But you're no man, Barty Gunliffe! You're not half a man."

Nevertheless, Bartholomew Gunliffe was a very fine young fellow, as far as the eye went. He was about five feet eight inches high, with strong arms and legs, with light curly brown hair and blue eyes. His father was but in a small way as a farmer, but, nevertheless, Barty Gunliffe was well thought of among the girls around. Everybody liked Barty,—excepting only Mally Trenglos, and she hated him like poison.

Barty, when he was asked why so good-natured a lad

as he persecuted a poor girl and an old man, threw himself upon the justice of the thing. It wouldn't do at all, according to his view, that any single person should take upon himself to own that which God Almighty sent as the common property of all. He would do Mally no harm, and so he had told her. But Mally was a vixen,— a wicked little vixen; and she must be taught to have a civil tongue in her head. When once Mally would speak him civil as he went for weed, he would get his father to pay the old man some sort of toll for the use of the path.

" Speak him civil?" said Mally. " Never; not while I have a tongue in my mouth!" And I fear old Glos encouraged her rather than otherwise in her view of the matter.

But her grandfather did not encourage her to hamstring the pony. Hamstringing a pony would be a serious thing, and old Glos thought it might be very awkward for both of them if Mally were put into prison. He suggested, therefore, that all manner of impediments should be put in the way of the pony's feet, surmising that the well-trained donkey might be able to work in spite of them. And Barty Gunliffe, on his next descent, did find the passage very awkward when he came near to Malachi's hut, but he made his way down, and poor Mally saw the lumps of rock at which she had laboured so hard pushed on one side or rolled out of the way with a steady persistency of injury towards herself that almost drove her frantic.

" Well, Barty, you're a nice boy," said old Glos, sitting in the doorway of the hut, as he watched the intruder.

" I ain't a doing no harm to none as doesn't harm me," said Barty. " The sea's free to all, Malachi."

"And the sky's free to all, but I musn't get up on the top of your big barn to look at it," said Mally, who was standing among the rocks with a long hook in her hand. The long hook was the tool with which she worked in dragging the weed from the waves. "But you ain't got no justice nor yet no sperrit, or you wouldn't come here to vex an old man like he."

"I didn't want to vex him, nor yet to vex you, Mally. You let me be for a while, and we'll be friends yet."

"Friends!" exclaimed Mally. "Who'd have the likes of you for a friend? What are you moving them stones for? Them stones belongs to grandfather." And in her wrath she made a movement as though she were going to fly at him.

"Let him be, Mally," said the old man; "let him be. He'll get his punishment. He'll come to be drowned some day if he comes down here when the wind is in shore."

"That he may be drowned then!" said Mally, in her anger. "If he was in the big hole there among the rocks, and the sea running in at half tide, I wouldn't lift a hand to help him out."

"Yes, you would, Mally; you'd fish me up with your hook like a big stick of seaweed."

She turned from him with scorn as he said this, and went into the hut. It was time for her to get ready for her work, and one of the great injuries done her lay in this,—that such a one as Barty Gunliffe should come and look at her during her toil among the breakers.

It was an afternoon in April, and the hour was something after four o'clock. There had been a heavy wind from the north-west all the morning, with gusts of rain, and the seagulls had been in and out of the cove all the

day, which was a sure sign to Mally that the incoming
tide would cover the rocks with weed.

The quick waves were now returning with wonderful
celerity over the low reefs, and the time had come at
which the treasure must be seized, if it was to be gar-
nered on that day. By seven o'clock it would be growing
dark, at nine it would be high water, and before daylight
the crop would be carried out again if not collected. All
this Mally understood very well, and some of this Barty
was beginning to understand also.

As Mally came down with her bare feet, bearing her
long hook in her hand, she saw Barty's pony standing
patiently on the sand, and in her heart she longed to
attack the brute. Barty at this moment, with a common
three-pronged fork in his hand, was standing down on
a large rock, gazing forth towards the waters. He had
declared that he would gather the weed only at places
which were inaccessible to Mally, and he was looking
out that he might settle where he would begin.

"Let 'un be, let 'un be," shouted the old man to
Mally, as he saw her take a step towards the beast, which
she hated almost as much as she hated the man.

Hearing her grandfather's voice through the wind,
she desisted from her purpose, if any purpose she had
had, and went forth to her work. As she passed down
the cove, and scrambled in among the rocks, she saw
Barty still standing on his perch; out beyond, the white-
curling waves were cresting and breaking themselves
with violence, and the wind was howling among the
caverns and abutments of the cliff.

Every now and then there came a squall of rain, and
though there was sufficient light, the heavens were black
with clouds. A scene more beautiful might hardly be

found by those who love the glories of the coast. The
light for such objects was perfect. Nothing could exceed
the grandeur of the colours,—the blue of the open sea,
the white of the breaking waves, the yellow sands, or the
streaks of red and brown which gave such richness to
the cliff.

But neither Mally nor Barty were thinking of such
things as these. Indeed they were hardly thinking of
their trade after its ordinary forms. Barty was meditating
how he might best accomplish his purpose of working
beyond the reach of Mally's feminine powers, and Mally
was resolving that wherever Barty went she would go
farther.

And, in many respects, Mally had the advantage.
She knew every rock in the spot, and was sure of those
which gave a good foothold, and sure also of those which
did not. And then her activity had been made perfect
by practice for the purpose to which it was to be devoted.
Barty, no doubt, was stronger than she, and quite as
active. But Barty could not jump among the waves from
one stone to another as she could do, nor was he as yet
able to get aid in his work from the very force of the
water as she could get it. She had been hunting seaweed
in that cove since she had been an urchin of six years
old, and she knew every hole and corner and every spot
of vantage. The waves were her friends, and she could
use them. She could measure their strength, and knew
when and where it would cease.

Mally was great down in the salt pools of her own
cove,—great, and very fearless. As she watched Barty
make his way forward from rock to rock, she told herself,
gleefully, that he was going astray. The curl of the wind
as it blew into the cove would not carry the weed up to the

northern buttresses of the cove; and then there was the great hole just there,—the great hole of which she had spoken when she wished him evil.

And now she went to work, hooking up the dishevelled hairs of the ocean, and landing many a cargo on the extreme margin of the sand, from whence she would be able in the evening to drag it back before the invading waters would return to reclaim the spoil.

And on his side also Barty made his heap up against the northern buttresses of which I have spoken. Barty's heap became bigger and still bigger, so that he knew, let the pony work as he might, he could not take it all up that evening. But still it was not as large as Mally's heap. Mally's hook was better than his fork, and Mally's skill was better than his strength. And when he failed in some haul Mally would jeer him with a wild, weird laughter, and shriek to him through the wind that he was not half a man. At first he answered her with laughing words, but before long, as she boasted of her success and pointed to his failure, he became angry, and then he answered her no more. He became angry with himself, in that he missed so much of the plunder before him.

The broken sea was full of the long straggling growth which the waves had torn up from the bottom of the ocean, but the masses were carried past him, away from him,—nay, once or twice over him; and then Mally's weird voice would sound in his ear, jeering him. The gloom among the rocks was now becoming thicker and thicker, the tide was beating in with increased strength, and the gusts of wind came with quicker and greater violence. But still he worked on. While Mally worked he would work, and he would work for some time after she was driven in. He would not be beaten by a girl.

The great hole was now full of water, but of water which seemed to be boiling as though in a pot. And the pot was full of floating masses,—large treasures of sea-weed which were thrown to and fro upon its surface, but lying there so thick that one would seem almost able to rest upon it without sinking.

Mally knew well how useless it was to attempt to rescue aught from the fury of that boiling cauldron. The hole went in under the rocks, and the side of it towards the shore lay high, slippery, and steep. The hole, even at low water, was never empty; and Mally believed that there was no bottom to it. Fish thrown in there could escape out to the ocean, miles away,—so Mally in her softer moods would tell the visitors to the cove. She knew the hole well. Poulnadioul she was accustomed to call it; which was supposed, when translated, to mean that this was the hole of the Evil One. Never did Mally attempt to make her own of weed which had found its way into that pot.

But Barty Gunliffe knew no better, and she watched him as he endeavoured to steady himself on the treacher-ously slippery edge of the pool. He fixed himself there and made a haul, with some small success. How he managed it she hardly knew, but she stood still for a while watching him anxiously, and then she saw him slip. He slipped, and recovered himself;—slipped again, and again recovered himself.

" Barty, you fool!" she screamed; " if you get yourself pitched in there, you'll never come out no more."

Whether she simply wished to frighten him, or whether her heart relented and she had thought of his danger with

dismay, who shall say? She could not have told herself.
She hated him as much as ever,—but she could hardly
have wished to see him drowned before her eyes.

"You go on, and don't mind me," said he, speaking
in a hoarse, angry tone.

"Mind you!—who minds you?" retorted the girl.
And then she again prepared herself for her work.

But as she went down over the rocks with her long
hook balanced in her hands, she suddenly heard a splash,
and, turning quickly round, saw the body of her enemy
tumbling amidst the eddying waves in the pool. The
tide had now come up so far that every succeeding wave
washed into it and over it from the side nearest to the
sea, and then ran down again back from the rocks, as the
rolling wave receded, with a noise like the fall of a cataract.
And then, when the surplus water had retreated for a
moment, the surface of the pool would be partly calm,
though the fretting bubbles would still boil up and down,
and there was ever a simmer on the surface, as though,
in truth, the cauldron were heated. But this time of
comparative rest was but a moment, for the succeeding
breaker would come up almost as soon as the foam of
the preceding one had gone, and then again the waters
would be dashed upon the rocks, and the sides would
echo with the roar of the angry wave.

Instantly Mally hurried across to the edge of the pool,
crouching down upon her hands and knees for security
as she did so. As a wave receded, Barty's head and face
was carried round near to her, and she could see that his
forehead was covered with blood. Whether he were alive
or dead she did not know. She had seen nothing but his
blood, and the light-coloured hair of his head lying
amidst the foam. Then his body was drawn along by

the suction of the retreating wave; but the mass of water
that escaped was not on this occasion large enough to
carry the man out with it.

Instantly Mally was at work with her hook, and getting it fixed into his coat, dragged him towards the spot
on which she was kneeling. During the half minute of
repose she got him so close that she could touch his
shoulder. Straining herself down, laying herself over the
long bending handle of the hook, she strove to grasp him
with her right hand. But she could not do it; she could
only touch him.

Then came the next breaker, forcing itself on with a
roar, looking to Mally as though it must certainly knock
her from her resting-place, and destroy them both. But
she had nothing for it but to kneel, and hold by her
hook.

What prayer passed through her mind at that moment
for herself or for him, or for that old man who was sitting
unconsciously up at the cabin, who can say? The great
wave came and rushed over her as she lay almost prostrate,
and when the water was gone from her eyes, and the
tumult of the foam, and the violence of the roaring
breaker had passed by her, she found herself at her
length upon the rock, while his body had been lifted up,
free from her hook, and was lying upon the slippery
ledge, half in the water and half out of it. As she
looked at him, in that instant, she could see that his
eyes were open and that he was struggling with his
hands.

"Hold by the hook, Barty," she cried, pushing the
stick of it before him, while she seized the collar of his
coat in her hands.

Had he been her brother, her lover, her father, she

could not have clung to him with more of the energy of despair. He did contrive to hold by the stick which she had given him, and when the succeeding wave had passed by, he was still on the ledge. In the next moment she was seated a yard or two above the hole, in comparative safety, while Barty lay upon the rocks with his still bleeding head resting upon her lap.

What could she do now? She could not carry him; and in fifteen minutes the sea would be up where she was sitting. He was quite insensible and very pale, and the blood was coming slowly,—very slowly,—from the wound on his forehead. Ever so gently she put her hand upon his hair to move it back from his face; and then she bent over his mouth to see if he breathed, and as she looked at him she knew that he was beautiful.

What would she not give that he might live? Nothing now was so precious to her as his life,—as this life which she had so far rescued from the waters. But what could she do? Her grandfather could scarcely get himself down over the rocks, if indeed he could succeed in doing so much as that. Could she drag the wounded man backwards, if it were only a few feet, so that he might lie above the reach of the waves till further assistance could be procured?

She set herself to work and she moved him, almost lifting him. As she did so she wondered at her own strength, but she was very strong at that moment. Slowly, tenderly, falling on the rocks herself so that he might fall on her, she got him back to the margin of the sand, to a spot which the waters would not reach for the next two hours.

Here her grandfather met them, having seen at last what had happened from the door.

" Dada," she said, " he fell into the pool yonder, and was battered against the rocks. See there at his forehead."

" Mally, I'm thinking that he's dead already," said old Glos, peering down over the body.

" No, dada; he is not dead; but mayhap he's dying. But I'll go at once up to the farm."

" Mally," said the old man, " look at his head. They'll say we murdered him."

" Who'll say so? Who'll lie like that? Didn't I pull him out of the hole?"

" What matters that? His father'll say we killed him."

It was manifest to Mally that whatever any one might say hereafter, her present course was plain before her. She must run up the path to Gunliffe's farm and get necessary assistance. If the world were as bad as her grandfather said, it would be so bad that she would not care to live longer in it. But be that as it might, there was no doubt as to what she must do now.

So away she went as fast as her naked feet could carry her up the cliff. When at the top she looked round to see if any person might be within ken, but she saw no one. So she ran with all her speed along the headland of the corn-field which led in the direction of old Gunliffe's house, and as she drew near to the homestead she saw that Barty's mother was leaning on the gate. As she approached, she attempted to call, but her breath failed her for any purpose of loud speech, so she ran on till she was able to grasp Mrs. Gunliffe by the arm.

" Where's himself?" she said, holding her hand upon her beating heart that she might husband her breath.

" Who is it you mean?" said Mrs. Gunliffe, who

participated in the family feud against Trenglos and his granddaughter. "What does the girl clutch me for in that way?"

"He's dying then, that's all."

"Who is dying? Is it old Malachi? If the old man's bad, we'll send some one down."

"It ain't dada, it's Barty! Where's himself? where's the master?" But by this time Mrs. Gunliffe was in an agony of despair, and was calling out for assistance lustily. Happily Gunliffe, the father, was at hand, and with him a man from the neighbouring village.

"Will you not send for the doctor?" said Mally. "Oh, man, you should send for the doctor!"

Whether any orders were given for the doctor she did not know, but in a very few minutes she was hurrying across the field again towards the path to the cove, and Gunliffe with the other man and his wife were following her.

As Mally went along she recovered her voice, for their step was not so quick as hers, and that which to them was a hurried movement, allowed her to get her breath again. And as she went she tried to explain to the father what had happened, saying but little, however, of her own doings in the matter. The wife hung behind listening, exclaiming every now and again that her boy was killed, and then asking wild questions as to his being yet alive. The father, as he went, said little. He was known as a silent, sober man, well spoken of for diligence and general conduct, but supposed to be stern and very hard when angered.

As they drew near to the top of the path, the other man whispered something to him, and then he turned round upon Mally and stopped her.

" If he has come by his death between you, your blood shall be taken for his," said he.

Then the wife shrieked out that her child had been murdered, and Mally, looking round into the faces of the three, saw that her grandfather's words had come true. They suspected her of having taken the life, in saving which she had nearly lost her own.

She looked round at them with awe in her face, and then, without saying a word, preceded them down the path. What had she to answer when such a charge as that was made against her? If they chose to say that she pushed him into the pool, and hit him with her hook as he lay amidst the waters, how could she show that it was not so?

Poor Mally knew little of the law of evidence, and it seemed to her that she was in their hands. But as she went down the steep track with a hurried step,—a step so quick that they could not keep up with her,—her heart was very full,—very full and very high. She had striven for the man's life as though he had been her brother. The blood was yet not dry on her own legs and arms, where she had torn them in his service. At one moment she had felt sure that she would die with him in that pool. And now they said that she had murdered him! It may be that he was not dead, and what would he say if ever he should speak again? Then she thought of that moment when his eyes had opened, and he had seemed to see her. She had no fear for herself, for her heart was very high. But it was full also,—full of scorn, disdain, and wrath.

When she had reached the bottom, she stood close to the door of the hut waiting for them, so that they might precede her to the other group, which was there in front of them, at a little distance on the sand.

"He is there, and dada is with him. Go and look at him," said Mally.

The father and mother ran on stumbling over the stones, but Mally remained behind by the door of the hut.

Barty Gunliffe was lying on the sand where Mally had left him, and old Malachi Trenglos was standing over him, resting himself with difficulty upon a stick.

"Not a move he's moved since she left him," said he, "not a move. I put his head on the old rug as you see, and I tried 'un with a drop of gin, but he wouldn't take it,—he wouldn't take it."

"Oh, my boy! my boy!" said the mother, throwing herself beside her son upon the sand.

"Haud your tongue, woman," said the father, kneeling down slowly by the lad's head, "whimpering that way will do 'un no good."

Then having gazed for a minute or two upon the pale face beneath him, he looked up sternly into that of Malachi Trenglos.

The old man hardly knew how to bear this terrible inquisition.

"He would come," said Malachi; "he brought it all upon hisself."

"Who was it struck him?" said the father.

"Sure he struck hisself, as he fell among the breakers."

"Liar!" said the father, looking up at the old man.

"They have murdered him!—they have murdered him!" shrieked the mother.

"Haud your peace, woman!" said the husband again. "They shall give us blood for blood."

Mally, leaning against the corner of the hovel, heard

it all, but did not stir. They might say what they liked. They might make it out to be murder. They might drag her and her grandfather to Camelford Gaol, and then to Bodmin, and the gallows; but they could not take from her the conscious feeling that was her own. She had done her best to save him,—her very best. And she had saved him!

She remembered her threat to him before they had gone down on the rocks together, and her evil wish. Those words had been very wicked; but since that she had risked her life to save his. They might say what they pleased of her, and do what they pleased. She knew what she knew.

Then the father raised his son's head and shoulders in his arms, and called on the others to assist him in carrying Barty towards the path. They raised him between them carefully and tenderly, and lifted their burden on towards the spot at which Mally was standing. She never moved, but watched them at their work; and the old man followed them, hobbling after them with his crutch.

When they had reached the end of the hut she looked upon Barty's face, and saw that it was very pale. There was no longer blood upon the forehead, but the great gash was to be seen there plainly, with its jagged cut, and the skin livid and blue round the orifice. His light brown hair was hanging back, as she had made it to hang when she had gathered it with her hand after the big wave had passed over them. Ah, how beautiful he was in Mally's eyes with that pale face, and the sad scar upon his brow! She turned her face away, that they might not see her tears; but she did not move, nor did she speak.

But now, when they had passed the end of the hut, shuffling along with their burden, she heard a sound which stirred her. She roused herself quickly from her leaning posture, and stretched forth her head as though to listen; then she moved to follow them. Yes, they had stopped at the bottom of the path, and had again laid the body on the rocks. She heard that sound again, as of a long, long sigh, and then, regardless of any of them, she ran to the wounded man's head.

" He is not dead," she said. " There; he is not dead."

As she spoke Barty's eyes opened, and he looked about him.

" Barty, my boy, speak to me," said the mother.

Barty turned his face upon his mother, smiled, and then stared about him wildly.

" How is it with thee, lad?" said his father. Then Barty turned his face again to the latter voice, and as he did so his eyes fell upon Mally.

" Mally!" he said, " Mally!"

It could have wanted nothing further to any of those present to teach them that, according to Barty's own view of the case, Mally had not been his enemy; and, in truth, Mally herself wanted no further triumph. That word had vindicated her, and she withdrew back to the hut.

" Dada," she said, " Barty is not dead, and I'm thinking they won't say anything more about our hurting him."

Old Glos shook his head. He was glad the lad hadn't met his death there; he didn't want the young man's blood, but he knew what folk would say. The poorer he was the more sure the world would be to trample on

him. Mally said what she could to comfort him, being
full of comfort herself.

She would have crept up to the farm if she dared, to
ask how Barty was. But her courage failed her when she
thought of that, so she went to work again, dragging back
the weed she had saved to the spot at which on the
morrow she would load the donkey. As she did this she
saw Barty's pony still standing patiently under the rock,
so she got a lock of fodder and threw it down before the
beast.

It had become dark down in the cove, but she was
still dragging back the seaweed, when she saw the glimmer
of a lantern coming down the pathway. It was a most
unusual sight, for lanterns were not common down in
Malachi's Cove. Down came the lantern rather slowly,—
much more slowly than she was in the habit of descending,
and then through the gloom she saw the figure of a man
standing at the bottom of the path. She went up to him,
and saw that it was Mr. Gunliffe, the father.

" Is that Mally?" said Gunliffe.

" Yes, it is Mally; and how is Barty, Mr. Gunliffe?"

" You must come to 'un yourself, now at once," said
the farmer. " He won't sleep a wink till he's seed you.
You must not say but you'll come."

" Sure I'll come if I'm wanted," said Mally.

Gunliffe waited a moment, thinking that Mally might
have to prepare herself, but Mally needed no preparation.
She was dripping with salt water from the weed which
she had been dragging, and her elfin locks were streaming wildly from her head; but, such as she was, she was
ready.

" Dada's in bed," she said, " and I can go now if you
please."

Then Gunliffe turned round and followed her up the
path, wondering at the life which this girl led so far
away from all her sex. It was now dark night, and he
had found her working at the very edge of the rolling
waves by herself, in the darkness, while the only human
being who might seem to be her protector had already
gone to his bed.

When they were at the top of the cliff Gunliffe took
her by her hand, and led her along. She did not comprehend this, but she made no attempt to take her hand
from his. Something he said about falling on the cliffs,
but it was muttered so lowly that Mally hardly understood him. But, in truth, the man knew that she had
saved his boy's life, and that he had injured her instead
of thanking her. He was now taking her to his heart,
and as words were wanting to him, he was showing his
love after this silent fashion. He held her by the hand
as though she were a child, and Mally tripped along at
his side asking him no questions.

When they were at the farm-yard gate, he stopped
there for a moment.

" Mally, my girl," he said, " he'll not be content till
he sees thee, but thou must not stay long wi' him, lass.
Doctor says he's weak like, and wants sleep badly."

Mally merely nodded her head, and then they entered
the house. Mally had never been within it before, and
looked about with wondering eyes at the furniture of
the big kitchen. Did any idea of her future destiny flash
upon her then, I wonder? But she did not pause here a
moment, but was led up to the bedroom above stairs,
where Barty was lying on his mother's bed.

" Is it Mally herself?" said the voice of the weak
youth.

" It's Mally herself," said the mother, " so now you can say what you please."

" Mally," said he, " Mally, it's along of you that I'm alive this moment."

" I'll not forget it on her," said the father, with his eyes turned away from her. " I'll never forget it on her."

" We hadn't a one but only him," said the mother, with her apron up to her face.

" Mally, you'll be friends with me now?" said Barty.

To have been made lady of the manor of the cove for ever, Mally couldn't have spoken a word now. It was not only that the words and presence of the people there cowed her and made her speechless, but the big bed, and the looking-glass, and the unheard-of wonders of the chamber, made her feel her own insignificance. But she crept up to Barty's side, and put her hand upon his.

" I'll come and get the weed, Mally; but it shall all be for you," said Barty.

" Indeed, you won't then, Barty dear," said the mother; " you'll never go near the awesome place again. What would we do if you were took from us?"

" He mustn't go near the hole if he does," said Mally, speaking at last in a solemn voice, and imparting the knowledge which she had kept to herself while Barty was her enemy; " 'specially not if the wind's any way from the nor'ard."

" She'd better go down now," said the father.

Barty kissed the hand which he held, and Mally, looking at him as he did so, thought that he was like an angel.

" You'll come and see us to-morrow, Mally," said he.

To this she made no answer, but followed Mrs. Gunliffe out of the room. When they were down in the kitchen, the mother had tea for her, and thick milk, and a hot cake,—all the delicacies which the farm could afford. I don't know that Mally cared much for the eating and drinking that night, but she began to think that the Gunliffes were good people,—very good people. It was better thus, at any rate, than being accused of murder and carried off to Camelford prison.

" I'll never forget it on her—never," the father had said.

Those words stuck to her from that moment, and seemed to sound in her ears all the night. How glad she was that Barty had come down to the cove,—oh, yes, how glad! There was no question of his dying now, and as for the blow on his forehead, what harm was that to a lad like him?

" But father shall go with you," said Mrs. Gunliffe, when Mally prepared to start for the cove by herself. Mally, however, would not hear of this. She could find her way to the cove whether it was light or dark.

" Mally, thou art my child now, and I shall think of thee so," said the mother, as the girl went off by herself.

Mally thought of this, too, as she walked home. How could she become Mrs. Gunliffe's child; ah, how?

I need not, I think, tell the tale any further. That Mally did become Mrs. Gunliffe's child, and how she became so the reader will understand; and in process of time the big kitchen and all the wonders of the farmhouse were her own. The people said that Barty Gunliffe had married a mermaid out of the sea; but when it was said in Mally's hearing I doubt whether she liked it; and when Barty himself would call her a mermaid she would frown at him, and throw about her black hair, and pretend to cuff him with her little hand.

Old Glos was brought up to the top of the cliff, and lived his few remaining days under the roof of Mr. Gunliffe's house; and as for the cove and the right of seaweed, from that time forth all that has been supposed to attach itself to Gunliffe's farm, and I do not know that any of the neighbours are prepared to dispute the right.

A Terribly Strange Bed

WILLIAM WILKIE COLLINS

William Wilkie Collins was born in London in 1824 and died there in 1889. After spending some years in business he was, in 1851, called to the bar, but he shortly afterwards decided to make literature his profession. His first published work was a biography of his father (1848), and his most famous novels are *The Woman in White* (1860), *No Name* (1862), and *The Moonstone* (1868). Collins, who was a close friend of Charles Dickens, excelled in melodrama, and was one of the first writers of detective stories and " thrillers " in the modern style.

Shortly after my education at college was finished, I happened to be staying at Paris with an English friend. We were both young men then, and lived, I am afraid, rather a wild life, in the delightful city of our sojourn. One night we were idling about the neighbourhood of the Palais Royal, doubtful to what amusement we should next betake ourselves. My friend proposed a visit to Frascati's; but his suggestion was not to my taste. I knew Frascati's, as the French saying is, by heart; had lost and won plenty of five-franc pieces there, merely for amusement's sake, until it was amusement no longer, and was thoroughly tired, in fact, of all the ghastly respectabilities of such a social anomaly as a respectable gambling-house.

" For Heaven's sake," said I to my friend, " let us go somewhere where we can see a little genuine, blackguard, poverty-stricken gaming, with no false gingerbread glitter thrown over it at all. Let us get away from fashion-able Frascati's, to a house where they don't mind letting in a man with a ragged coat, or a man with no coat, ragged or otherwise."

" Very well," said my friend, " we needn't go out of the Palais Royal to find the sort of company you want. Here's the place just before us; as blackguard a place, by all report, as you could possibly wish to see."

In another minute we arrived at the door, and entered the house.

When we got upstairs, and had left our hats and sticks with the doorkeeper, we were admitted into the chief gambling-room. We did not find many people assembled there. But, few as the men were who looked up at us on our entrance, they were all types—lamentably true types —of their respective classes.

We had come to see blackguards; but these men were something worse. There is a comic side, more or less appreciable, in all blackguardism: here there was nothing but tragedy—mute, weird tragedy. The quiet in the room was horrible. The thin, haggard, long-haired young man, whose sunken eyes fiercely watched the turning up of the cards, never spoke; the flabby, fat-faced, pimply player, who pricked his piece of pasteboard perseveringly, to register how often black won, and how often red, never spoke; the dirty, wrinkled old man, with the vulture eyes and the darned great-coat, who had lost his last sou, and still looked on desperately after he could play no longer, never spoke. Even the voice of the croupier sounded as if it were strangely dulled and thickened in the atmosphere of the room. I had entered the place to laugh, but the spectacle before me was something to weep over. I soon found it necessary to take refuge in excitement from the depression of spirits which was fast stealing on me. Unfortunately I sought the nearest excitement, by going to the table and beginning to play. Still more unfortunately, as the event will show, I won— won prodigiously; won incredibly; won at such a rate that the regular players at the table crowded round me; and staring at my stakes with hungry, superstitious eyes, whispered to one another that the English stranger was going to break the bank.

The game was Rouge et Noir. I had played at it in every city in Europe, without, however, the care or the wish to study the Theory of Chances—that philosopher's stone of all gamblers! And a gambler, in the strict sense of the word, I had never been. I was heart-whole from the corroding passion for play. My gaming was a mere idle amusement. I never resorted to it by necessity, because I never knew what it was to want money. I never practised it so incessantly as to lose more than I could afford, or to gain more than I could coolly pocket without being thrown off my balance by my good luck. In short, I had hitherto frequented gambling-tables— just as I frequented ball-rooms and opera-houses— because they amused me, and because I had nothing better to do with my leisure hours.

But on this occasion it was very different—now, for the first time in my life, I felt what the passion for play really was. My successes first bewildered, and then, in the most literal meaning of the word, intoxicated me. Incredible as it may appear, it is nevertheless true, that I only lost when I attempted to estimate chances, and

played according to previous calculation. If I left everything to luck, and staked without any care or consideration, I was sure to win—to win in the face of every
recognized probability in favour of the bank. At first
some of the men present ventured their money safely
enough on my colour; but I speedily increased my
stakes to sums which they dared not risk. One after
another they left off playing, and breathlessly looked on
at my game.

Still, time after time, I staked higher and higher, and
still won. The excitement in the room rose to fever pitch.
The silence was interrupted by a deep-muttered chorus
of oaths and exclamations in different languages, every
time the gold was shovelled across to my side of the table
—even the imperturbable croupier dashed his rake on
the floor in a (French) fury of astonishment at my success.
But one man present preserved his self-possession, and
that man was my friend. He came to my side, and whispering in English, begged me to leave the place, satisfied
with what I had already gained. I must do him the justice
to say that he repeated his warnings and entreaties several
times, and only left me and went away, after I had re-
jected his advice (I was to all intents and purposes gam-
bling drunk) in terms which rendered it impossible for
him to address me again that night.

Shortly after he had gone, a hoarse voice behind me
cried, " Permit me, my dear sir—permit me to restore
to their proper place, two napoleons which you have
dropped. Wonderful luck, sir! I pledge you my word
of honour, as an old soldier, in the course of my long
experience in this sort of thing, I never saw such luck as
yours—never! Go on, sir—*Sacre mille bombes!* Go on
boldly, and break the bank!"

I turned round and saw, nodding and smiling at me with inveterate civility, a tall man, dressed in a frogged and braided surtout.

If I had been in my senses, I should have considered him, personally, as being rather a suspicious specimen of an old soldier. He had goggling, bloodshot eyes, mangy moustaches, and a broken nose. His voice betrayed a barrack-room intonation of the worst order, and he had the dirtiest pair of hands I ever saw—even in France. These little personal peculiarities exercised, however, no repelling influence on me. In the mad excitement, the reckless triumph of that moment, I was ready to " fraternize " with anybody who encouraged me in my game. I accepted the old soldier's offered pinch of snuff; clapped him on the back, and swore he was the honestest fellow in the world—the most glorious relic of the Grand Army that I had ever met with. " Go on!" cried my military friend, snapping his fingers in ecstasy—" Go on, and win! Break the bank—*Mille tonnerres!* my gallant English comrade, break the bank!"

And I *did* go on—went on at such a rate, that in another quarter of an hour the croupier called out, " Gentlemen, the bank has discontinued for to-night." All the notes, and all the gold in that " bank ", now lay in a heap under my hands; the whole floating capital of the gambling-house was waiting to pour into my pockets!

" Tie up the money in your pocket-handkerchief, my worthy sir," said the old soldier, as I wildly plunged my hands into my heap of gold. " Tie it up, as we used to tie up a bit of dinner in the Grand Army; your winnings are too heavy for any breeches-pockets that ever were sewed. There! that's it—shovel them in, notes and all! *Credie!* what luck! Stop! another napoleon on the floor.

Ah! sacre petit polisson de Napoleon! have I found thee at last? Now then, sir—two tight double knots each way with your honourable permission, and the money's safe. Feel it! feel it, fortunate sir! hard and round as a cannon-ball— *À bas* if they had only fired such cannon-balls at us at Austerlitz—*nom d'une pipe!* if they only had! And now, as an ancient grenadier, as an ex-brave of the French army, what remains for me to do? I ask what? Simply this, to entreat my valued English friend to drink a bottle of champagne with me, and toast the goddess Fortune in foaming goblets before we part!"

" Excellent ex-brave! Convivial ancient grenadier! Champagne by all means! An English cheer for an old soldier! Hurrah! hurrah! Another English cheer for the goddess Fortune! Hurrah! hurrah! hurrah!"

" Bravo! the Englishman; the amiable, gracious Englishman, in whose veins circulates the vivacious blood of France! Another glass? *À bas!*—the bottle is empty! Never mind! *Vive le vin!* I, the old soldier, order another bottle, and half a pound of *bonbons* with it!"

" No, no, ex-brave; never—ancient grenadier! *Your* bottle last time; *my* bottle this! Behold it! Toast away! The French Army! the great Napoleon! the present company! the croupier! the honest croupier's wife and daughters—if he has any! the ladies generally! everybody in the world!"

By the time the second bottle of champagne was emptied, I felt as if I had been drinking liquid fire—my brain seemed all aflame. No excess in wine had ever had this effect on me before in my life. Was it the result of a stimulant acting upon my system when I was in a highly excited state? Was my stomach in a particularly disordered condition? Or was the champagne amazingly strong?

" Ex-brave of the French Army!" cried I, in ὶ mad
state of exhilaration, " *I* am on fire! how are *you*? You
have set me on fire! Do you hear, my hero of Austerlitz?
Let us have a third bottle of champagne to put the flame
out!"

The old soldier wagged his head, rolled his goggle-
eyes, until I expected to see them slip out of their sockets;
placed his dirty forefinger by the side of his broken nose;
solemnly ejaculated " Coffee!" and immediately ran off
into an inner room.

The word pronounced by the eccentric veteran seemed
to have a magical effect on the rest of the company present.
With one accord they all rose to depart. Probably they
had expected to profit by my intoxication; but finding
that my new friend was benevolently bent on preventing
me from getting dead drunk, had now abandoned all
hope of thriving pleasantly on my winnings. Whatever
their motive might be, at any rate they went away in a
body. When the old soldier returned and sat down
again opposite to me at the table, we had the room to
ourselves. I could see the croupier, in a sort of vestibule
which opened out of it, eating his supper in solitude.
The silence was now deeper than ever.

A sudden change, too, had come over the " ex-brave ".
He assumed a portentously solemn look; and when he
spoke to me again, his speech was ornamented by no
oaths, enforced by no finger-snapping, enlivened by no
apostrophes or exclamations.

" Listen, my dear sir," said he, in mysteriously con-
fidential tones—" listen to an old soldier's advice. I
have been to the mistress of the house (a very charming
woman, with a genius for cookery!) to impress on her
the necessity of making us some particularly strong and

good coffee. You must drink this coffee in order to get rid of your little amiable exaltation of spirits before you think of going home—you *must*, my good and gracious friend! With all that money to take home to-night, it is a sacred duty to yourself to have your wits about you. You are known to be a winner to an enormous extent by several gentlemen present to-night, who, in a certain point of view, are very worthy and excellent fellows; but they are mortal men, my dear sir, and they have their amiable weaknesses! Need I say more? Ah, no, no! you understand me! Now, this is what you must do —send for a cabriolet when you feel quite well again— draw up all the windows when you get into it—and tell the driver to take you home only through the large and well-lighted thoroughfares. Do this; and you and your money will be safe. Do this; and to-morrow you will thank an old soldier for giving you a word of honest advice."

Just as the ex-brave ended his oration in very lachrymose tones, the coffee came in, ready poured out in two cups. My attentive friend handed me one of the cups with a bow. I was parched with thirst, and drank it off at a draft. Almost instantly afterward I was seized with a fit of giddiness, and felt more completely intoxicated than ever. The room whirled round and round furiously; the old soldier seemed to be regularly bobbing up and down before me like the piston of a steam-engine. I was half deafened by a violent singing in my ears; a feeling of utter bewilderment, helplessness, idiocy, overcame me. I rose from my chair, holding on by the table to keep my balance; and stammered out that I felt dreadfully unwell—so unwell that I did not know how I was to get home.

" My dear friend," answered the old soldier—and even his voice seemed to be bobbing up and down as he spoke—" my dear friend, it would be madness to go home in *your* state; you would be sure to lose your money; you might be robbed and murdered with the greatest ease. *I* am going to sleep here: *do* you sleep here, too— they make up capital beds in this house—take one; sleep off the effects of the wine, and go home safely with your winnings to-morrow—to-morrow, in broad daylight."

I had but two ideas left: one, that I must never let go hold of my handkerchief full of money; the other, that I must lie down somewhere immediately, and fall off into a comfortable sleep. So I agreed to the proposal about the bed, and took the offered arm of the old soldier, carrying my money with my disengaged hand. Preceded by the croupier, we passed along some passages and up a flight of stairs into the bedroom which I was to occupy. The ex-brave shook me warmly by the hand, proposed that we should breakfast together, and then, followed by the croupier, left me for the night.

I ran to the wash-hand stand; drank some of the water in my jug; poured the rest out, and plunged my face into it; then sat down in a chair and tried to compose myself. I soon felt better. The change for my lungs, from the fetid atmosphere of the gambling-house to the cool air of the apartment I now occupied, the almost equally refreshing change for my eyes, from the glaring gaslights of the " salon " to the dim, quiet flicker of one bedroom-candle, aided wonderfully the restorative effects of cold water. The giddiness left me, and I began to feel a little like a reasonable being again. My first thought was of the risk of sleeping all night in a gambling-house; my second, of the still greater risk of trying to get out after the house was closed, and of going home alone at night through the streets of Paris with a large sum of money about me. I had slept in worse places than this on my travels; so I determined to lock, bolt, and barricade my door, and take my chance till the next morning.

Accordingly, I secured myself against all intrusion; looked under the bed, and into the cupboard; tried the fastening of the window; and then, satisfied that I had taken every proper precaution, pulled off my upper clothing, put my light, which was a dim one, on the hearth among a feathery litter of wood-ashes, and got into bed, with the handkerchief full of money under my pillow.

I soon felt not only that I could not go to sleep, but that I could not even close my eyes. I was wide awake, and in a high fever. Every nerve in my body trembled— every one of my senses seemed to be preternaturally sharpened. I tossed and rolled, and tried every kind of position and perseveringly sought out the cold corners of the bed, and all to no purpose. Now I thrust my arms over the clothes; now I poked them under the clothes; now I violently shot my legs straight out down to the bottom of the bed; now I convulsively coiled them up as near my chin as they would go; now I shook out my crumpled pillow, changed it to the cool side, patted it flat, and lay down quietly on my back; now I fiercely doubled it in two, set it up on end, thrust it against the board of the bed, and tried a sitting posture. Every effort was in vain; I groaned with vexation as I felt that I was in for a sleepless night.

What could I do? I had no book to read. And yet, unless I found out some method of diverting my mind, I felt certain that I was in the condition to imagine all

sorts of horrors; to rack my brain with forebodings of
every possible and impossible danger; in short, to pass
the night in suffering all conceivable varieties of nervous
terror.

I raised myself on my elbow, and looked about the
room—which was brightened by a lovely moonlight pour-
ing straight through the window—to see if it contained
any pictures of ornaments that I could at all clearly distinguish. While my eyes wandered from wall to wall,
a remembrance of Le Maistre's delightful little book,
Voyage autour de ma Chambre, occurred to me. I resolved
to imitate the French author, and find occupation and
amusement enough to relieve the tedium of my wakeful-
ness, by making a mental inventory of every article of
furniture I could see, and by following up to their sources
the multitude of associations which even a chair, a table,
or a wash-hand stand may be made to call forth.

In the nervous, unsettled state of my mind at that
moment, I found it much easier to make my inventory
than to make my reflections, and thereupon soon gave up
all hope of thinking in Le Maistre's fanciful track—or,
indeed, of thinking at all. I looked about the room at the
different articles of furniture, and did nothing more.

There was, first, the bed I was lying in; a four-post
bed, of all things in the world to meet with in Paris—yes,
a thorough clumsy British four-poster, with a regular
top lined with chintz—the regular fringed valance all
round—the regular stifling, unwholesome curtains, which
I remembered having mechanically drawn back against
the posts without particularly noticing the bed when I first
got into the room. Then there was the marble-topped
wash-hand stand, from which the water I had spilled, in
my hurry to pour it out, was still dripping, slowly and

more slowly, on to the brick floor. Then two small chairs, with my coat, waistcoat, and trousers flung on them. Then a large elbow-chair covered with dirty white dimity, with my cravat and shirt collar thrown over the back. Then a chest of drawers with two of the brass handles off, and a tawdry, broken china inkstand placed on it by way of ornament for the top. Then the dressing-table, adorned by a very small looking-glass, and a very large pincushion. Then the window—an unusually large window. Then a dark old picture, which the feeble candle dimly showed me. It was the picture of a fellow in a high Spanish hat, crowned with a plume of towering feathers. A swarthy, sinister ruffian, looking upward, shading his eyes with his hand, and looking intently upward—it might be at some tall gallows on which he was going to be hanged. At any rate, he had the appearance of thoroughly deserving it.

This picture put a kind of constraint upon me to look upward too—at the top of the bed. It was a gloomy and not an interesting object, and I looked back at the picture. I counted the feathers in the man's hat—they stood out in relief—three white, two green. I observed the crown of his hat, which was of a conical shape, according to the fashion supposed to have been favoured by Guido Fawkes. I wondered what he was looking up at. It couldn't be at the stars; such a desperado was neither astrologer nor astronomer. It must be at the high gallows, and he was going to be hanged presently. Would the executioner come into possession of his conical hat and plume of feathers? I counted the feathers again—three white, two green.

While I still lingered over this very improving and intellectual employment, my thoughts insensibly began

to wander. The moonlight shining into the room reminded me of a certain moonlight night in England—
the night after a picnic party in a Welsh valley. Every
incident of the drive homeward, through lovely scenery,
which the moonlight made lovelier than ever, came back
to my remembrance, though I had never given the picnic
a thought for years; though, if I had *tried* to recollect
it, I could certainly have recalled little or nothing of
that scene long past. Of all the wonderful faculties that
help to tell us we are immortal, which speaks the sublime
truth more eloquently than memory? Here was I, in a
strange house of the most suspicious character, in a situation of uncertainty, and even of peril, which might seem to
make the cool exercise of my recollection almost out of
the question; nevertheless, remembering, quite involuntarily, places, people, conversations, minute circumstances of every kind, which I had thought forgotten
forever; which I could not possibly have recalled at
will, even under the most favourable auspices. And
what cause had produced in a moment the whole of this
strange, complicated, mysterious effect? Nothing but
some rays of moonlight shining in at my bedroom window.

I was still thinking of the picnic—of our merriment on
the drive home—of the sentimental young lady who
would quote *Childe Harold* because it was moonlight.
I was absorbed by these past scenes and past amusements,
when, in an instant, the thread on which my memories
hung snapped asunder; my attention immediately came
back to present things more vividly than ever, and I
found myself, I neither knew why nor wherefore, looking
hard at the picture again.

Looking for what?

Good God! the man had pulled his hat down on his

brows! No! the hat itself was gone! Where was the conical crown? Where the feathers—three white, two green? Not there! In place of the hat and feathers, what dusky object was it that now hid his forehead, his eyes, his shading hand?

Was the bed moving?

I turned on my back and looked up. Was I mad? drunk? dreaming? giddy again? or was the top of the bed really moving down—sinking slowly, regularly, silently, horribly, right down throughout the whole of its length and breadth—right down upon me, as I lay underneath?

My blood seemed to stand still. A deadly, paralysing coldness stole all over me as I turned my head round on the pillow and determined to test whether the bed-top was really moving or not, by keeping my eye on the man in the picture.

The next look in that direction was enough. The dull, black, frowsy outline of the valance above me was within an inch of being parallel with his waist. I still looked breathlessly. And steadily and slowly—very slowly— I saw the figure, and the line of frame below the figure, vanish, as the valance moved down before it.

I am, constitutionally, anything but timid. I have been on more than one occasion in peril of my life, and have not lost my self-possession for an instant; but when the conviction first settled on my mind that the bed-top was really moving, was steadily and continuously sinking down upon me, I looked up shuddering, helpless, panic-stricken, beneath the hideous machinery for murder, which was advancing closer and closer to suffocate me where I lay.

I looked up, motionless, speechless, breathless. The

candle, fully spent, went out; but the moonlight still brightened the room. Down and down, without pausing and without sounding, came the bed-top, and still my panic terror seemed to bind me faster and faster to the mattress on which I lay—down and down it sank, till the dusty odour from the lining of the canopy came stealing into my nostrils.

At that final moment the instinct of self-preservation startled me out of my trance, and I moved at last. There was just room for me to roll myself sidewise off the bed. As I dropped noiselessly to the floor, the edge of the murderous canopy touched me on the shoulder.

Without stopping to draw my breath, without wiping the cold sweat from my face, I rose instantly on my knees to watch the bed-top. I was literally spellbound by it. If I had heard footsteps behind me, I could not have turned round; if a means of escape had been miraculously provided for me, I could not have moved to take advantage of it. The whole life in me was, at that moment, concentrated in my eyes.

It descended—the whole canopy, with the fringe round it, came down—down—close down; so close that there was not room now to squeeze my finger between the bed-top and the bed. I felt at the sides, and discovered that what had appeared to me from beneath to be the ordinary light canopy of a four-post bed was in reality a thick, broad mattress, the substance of which was concealed by the valance and its fringe. I looked up and saw the four posts rising hideously bare. In the middle of the bed-top was a huge wooden screw that had evidently worked it down through a hole in the ceiling, just as ordinary presses are worked down on the substance selected for compression. The frightful apparatus moved without making the faintest noise. There had been no creaking as it came down; there was now not the faintest sound from the room above. Amidst a dead and awful silence I beheld before me—in the Nineteenth Century, and in the civilized capital of France—such a machine for secret murder by suffocation as might have existed in the worst days of the Inquisition, in the lonely inns among the Hartz Mountains, in the mysterious tribunals of Westphalia! Still, as I looked on it, I could not move, I could hardly breathe, but I began to recover the power of thinking, and in a moment I discovered the murderous conspiracy framed against me in all its horror.

My cup of coffee had been drugged, and drugged too strongly. I had been saved from being smothered by having taken an overdose of some narcotic. How I had chafed and fretted at the fever fit which had preserved my life by keeping me awake! How recklessly I had confided myself to the two wretches who had led me into this room, determined, for the sake of my winnings, to kill me in my sleep by the surest and most horrible contrivance for secretly accomplishing my destruction! How many men, winners like me, had slept, as I had proposed to sleep, in that bed, and had never been seen or heard of more! I shuddered at the bare idea of it.

But ere long all thought was again suspended by the sight of the murderous canopy moving once more. After it had remained on the bed—as nearly as I could guess—about ten minutes, it began to move up again. The villains who worked it from above evidently believed that their purpose was now accomplished. Slowly and silently, as it had descended, that horrible bed-top rose toward its former place. When it reached the upper extremities of the four posts, it reached the ceiling too. Neither hole nor screw could be seen; the bed became in appearance an ordinary bed again—the canopy an ordinary canopy—even to the most suspicious eyes.

Now, for the first time, I was able to move—to rise from my knees—to dress myself in my upper clothing—and to consider of how I should escape. If I betrayed by the smallest noise that the attempt to suffocate me had failed, I was certain to be murdered. Had I made any noise already? I listened intently, looking toward the door.

No! No footsteps in the passage outside—no sound of a tread, light or heavy, in the room above—absolute silence everywhere. Besides locking and bolting my door, I had moved an old wooden chest against it, which I had found under the bed. To remove this chest (my blood ran cold as I thought of what its contents *might* be!) without making some disturbance was impossible; and, moreover, to think of escaping through the house, now barred up for the night, was sheer insanity. Only one chance was left me—the window. I stole to it on tiptoe.

My bedroom was on the first floor, above an entresol, and looked into the back street. I raised my hand to open the window, knowing that on that action hung, by the merest hair-breadth, my chance of safety. They keep vigilant watch in a House of Murder. If any part of the frame cracked, if the hinge creaked, I was a lost man! It must have occupied me at least five minutes, reckoning by time—five *hours* reckoning by suspense—to open that window. I succeeded in doing it silently—in doing it with all the dexterity of a house-breaker—and then looked down into the street. To leap the distance beneath me would be almost certain destruction! Next, I looked round at the sides of the house. Down the left side ran a thick water-pipe—it passed close by the outer edge of the window. The moment I saw the pipe, I knew I was saved. My breath came and went freely for the first time since I had seen the canopy of the bed moving down upon me!

To some men the means of escape which I had discovered might have seemed difficult and dangerous enough—to *me* the prospect of slipping down the pipe into the street did not suggest even a thought of peril. I had always been accustomed, by the practice of gymnastics, to keep up my schoolboy powers as a daring and expert climber; and knew that my head, hands, and feet would serve me faithfully in any hazards of ascent or descent. I had already got one leg over the window-sill, when I remembered the handkerchief filled with money under my pillow. I could well have afforded to leave it behind me, but I was revengefully determined that the miscreants of the gambling-house should miss their plunder as well as their victim. So I went back to the bed and tied the heavy handkerchief at my back by my cravat.

Just as I had made it tight and fixed it in a comfortable place, I thought I heard a sound of breathing outside the door. The chill feeling of horror ran through me again as I listened. No! Dead silence still in the passage—I had only heard the night air blowing softly into the room. The next moment I was on the window-sill—and the next I had a firm grip on the water-pipe with my hands and knees.

I slid down into the street easily and quietly, as I thought I should, and immediately set off at the top of

my speed to a branch " Prefecture " of Police, which
I knew was situated in the immediate neighbourhood.
A " Sub-prefect ", and several picked men among his
subordinates, happened to be up, maturing, I believe,
some scheme for discovering the perpetrator of a mysterious murder which all Paris was talking of just then.
When I began my story, in a breathless hurry and in very
bad French, I could see that the Sub-prefect suspected
me of being a drunken Englishman who had robbed
somebody; but he soon altered his opinion as I went on,
and before I had anything like concluded, he shoved all
the papers before him into a drawer, put on his hat,
supplied me with another (for I was bareheaded), ordered
a file of soldiers, desired his expert followers to get ready
all sorts of tools for breaking open doors and ripping up
brick flooring, and took my arm, in the most friendly
and familiar manner possible, to lead me with him out
of the house. I will venture to say that when the Sub-
prefect was a little boy, and was taken for the first time
to the play, he was not half as much pleased as he was
now at the job in prospect for him at the gambling-
house!

Away we went through the streets, the Sub-prefect
cross-examining and congratulating me in the same
breath as we marched at the head of our formidable *posse
comitatus*. Sentinels were placed at the back and front
of the house the moment we got to it, a tremendous
battery of knocks was directed against the door; a light
appeared at a window; I was told to conceal myself
behind the police—then came more knocks, and a cry
of " Open in the name of the law!" At that terrible
summons bolts and locks gave way before an invisible
hand, and the moment after the Sub-prefect was in the

passage, confronting a waiter half dressed and ghastly pale. This was the short dialogue which immediately took place:

" We want to see the Englishman who is sleeping in this house?"

" He went away hours ago."

" He did no such thing. His friend went away; *he* remained. Show us to his bedroom!"

" I swear to you, Monsieur le Sous-prefet, he is not here! He——"

" I swear to you, Monsieur le Garçon, he is. He slept here—he didn't find your bed comfortable—he came to us to complain of it—here he is among my men—and here am I ready to look for a flea or two in his bedstead. Renaudin!" (calling to one of the subordinates, and pointing to the waiter), " collar that man, and tie his hands behind him. Now, then, gentlemen, let us walk upstairs!"

Every man and woman in the house was secured—the " Old Soldier " the first. Then I identified the bed in which I had slept, and then we went into the room above.

No object that was at all extraordinary appeared in any part of it. The Sub-prefect looked round the place, commanded everybody to be silent, stamped twice on the floor, called for a candle, looked attentively at the spot he had stamped on, and ordered the flooring there to be carefully taken up. This was done in no time. Lights were produced, and we saw a deep raftered cavity between the floor of this room and the ceiling of the room beneath. Through this cavity there ran perpendicularly a sort of case of iron thickly greased; and inside the case appeared the screw, which communicated with the bed-top below. Extra lengths of screw, freshly oiled; levers covered with felt; all the complete upper works of a heavy press—constructed with infernal ingenuity so as to join the fixtures below, and when taken to pieces again to go into the smallest possible compass—were next discovered and pulled out on the floor. After some little difficulty the Sub-prefect succeeded in putting the machinery together, and, leaving his men to work it, descended with me to the bedroom. The smothering canopy was then lowered, but not so noiselessly as I had seen it lowered. When I mentioned this to the Sub-prefect, his answer, simple as it was, had a terrible significance. " My men," said he, " are working down the bed-top for the first time—the men whose money you won were in better practice."

We left the house in the sole possession of two police agents—every one of the inmates being removed to prison on the spot. The Sub-prefect, after taking down my " procès verbal " in his office, returned with me to my hotel to get my passport. " Do you think," I asked, as I gave it to him, " that any men have really been smothered in that bed, as they tried to smother *me*?"

" I have seen dozens of drowned men laid out at the Morgue," answered the Sub-prefect, " in whose pocket-books were found letters stating that they had committed suicide in the Seine, because they had lost everything at the gaming-table. Do I know how many of those men entered the same gambling-house that *you* entered? won as *you* won? took that bed as *you* took it? slept in it? were smothered in it? and were privately thrown into the river, with a letter of explanation written by the murderers and placed in their pocket-books? No man

can say how many or how few have suffered the fate
from which you have escaped. The people of the gambling-
house kept their bedstead machinery a secret from us—
even from the police! The dead kept the rest of the secret
for them. Good-night, or rather good-morning, Monsieur
Faulkner! Be at my office again at nine o'clock—in the
meantime, au revoir!"

The rest of my story is soon told. I was examined and
re-examined; the gambling-house was strictly searched
all through from top to bottom; the prisoners were
separately interrogated; and two of the less guilty among
them made a confession. I discovered that the Old
Soldier was the master of the gambling-house—*justice*
discovered that he had been drummed out of the army
as a vagabond years ago; that he had been guilty of all
sorts of villainies since; that he was in possession of
stolen property, which the owners identified; and that
he, the croupier, another accomplice, and the woman
who had made my cup of coffee, were all in the secret
of the bedstead. There appeared some reason to doubt
whether the inferior persons attached to the house knew
anything of the suffocating machinery; and they received
the benefit of that doubt, by being treated simply as
thieves and vagabonds. As for the Old Soldier and his
two head myrmidons, they went to the galleys; the
woman who had drugged my coffee was imprisoned for
I forget how many years; the regular attendants at the
gambling-house were considered " suspicious ", and
placed under " surveillance "; and I became, for one
whole week (which is a long time), the head " lion " in
Parisian society. My adventure was dramatized by three
illustrious play-makers, but never saw theatrical daylight; for the censorship forbade the introduction on

the stage of a correct copy of the gambling-house bedstead.

One good result was produced by my adventure, which any censorship must have approved: it cured me of ever again trying " Rouge et Noir " as an amusement. The sight of a green cloth, with packs of cards and heaps of money on it, will henceforth be forever associated in my mind with the sight of a bed canopy descending to suffocate me in the silence and darkness of the night.

The Iliad of Sandy Bar

FRANCIS BRET HARTE

Francis Bret Harte was born at Albany, New York, in 1839. At the age of fifteen he went to California, where he worked, amongst other things, as a teacher, printer, miner, and journalist. In 1868 he became editor of the *Overland Monthly*, to which he contributed some of his best short stories, such as *The Luck of Roaring Camp*, *Tennessee's Partner*, and *The Outcasts of Poker Flat*. He held consular posts in Germany from 1878 to 1880, and at Glasgow from 1880 to 1885, and from 1885 till his death in 1902 he resided in England. Harte published over forty books of stories, sketches, and verse, the best of them dealing with California in the early mining days. As a writer of short stories he is unsurpassed in constructive ability, in narrative power, and in describing, without sentimentality, situations of humour or pathos.

Before nine o'clock it was pretty well known all along the river that the two parties of the " Amity Claim " had quarrelled and separated at daybreak. At that time the attention of their nearest neighbour had been attracted by the sounds of altercations and two consecutive pistol-shots. Running out, he had seen, dimly, in the grey mist that rose from the river, the tall form of Scott, one of the partners, descending the hill toward the cañon; a moment later, York, the other partner, had appeared from the cabin, and walked in an opposite direction toward the river, passing within a few feet of the curious

198

watcher. Later it was discovered that a serious Chinaman, cutting wood before the cabin, had witnessed part of the quarrel. But John was stolid, indifferent, and reticent. " Me choppee wood, me no fightee," was his serene response to all anxious queries. " But what did they *say*, John?" John did not " *sabe* ". Colonel Starbottle deftly ran over the various popular epithets which a generous public sentiment might accept as reasonable provocation for an assault. But John did not recognize them. " And this yer's the cattle," said the Colonel, with some severity, " that some thinks oughter be allowed to testify agin' a White Man! Git—you heathen!"

Still the quarrel remained inexplicable. That two men, whose amiability and grave tact had earned for them the title of " The Peacemakers ", in a community not greatly given to the passive virtues—that these men, singularly devoted to each other, should suddenly and violently quarrel, might well excite the curiosity of the camp. A few of the more inquisitive visited the late scene of conflict, now deserted by its former occupants. There was no trace of disorder or confusion in the neat cabin. The rude table was arranged as if for breakfast; the pan of yellow biscuit still sat upon that hearth whose dead embers might have typified the evil passions that had raged there but an hour before. But Colonel Starbottle's eye—albeit, somewhat bloodshot and rheumy— was more intent on practical details. On examination, a bullet-hole was found in the doorpost, and another, nearly opposite, in the casing of the window. The Colonel called attention to the fact that the one " agreed with " the bore of Scott's revolver, and the other with that of York's derringer. " They must hev stood about yer," said the Colonel, taking position; " not mor'n three feet

apart, and—missed!" There was a fine touch of pathos
in the falling inflection of the Colonel's voice, which was
not without effect. A delicate perception of wasted
opportunity thrilled his auditors.

But the Bar was destined to experience a greater dis-
appointment. The two antagonists had not met since the
quarrel, and it was vaguely rumoured that, on the occasion
of a second meeting, each had determined to kill the
other " on sight ". There was, consequently, some
excitement—and, it is to be feared, no little gratification
—when, at ten o'clock, York stepped from the Magnolia
Saloon into the one, long straggling street of the camp,
at the same moment that Scott left the blacksmith's shop
at the forks of the road. It was evident, at a glance, that
a meeting could only be avoided by the actual retreat of
one or the other.

In an instant the doors and windows of the adjacent
saloons were filled with faces. Heads unaccountably
appeared above the river-banks and from behind boulders.
An empty wagon at the cross-road was suddenly crowded
with people, who seemed to have sprung from the earth.
There was much running and confusion on the hillside.
On the mountain-road, Mr. Jack Hamlin had reined up
his horse and was standing upright on the seat of his
buggy. And the two objects of this absorbing attention
approached each other.

" York's got the sun," " Scott'll line him on that
tree," " He's waiting to draw his fire," came from the
cart; and then it was silent. But above this human
breathlessness the river rushed and sang, and the wind
rustled the tree-tops with an indifference that seemed
obtrusive. Colonel Starbottle felt it, and, in a moment
of sublime preoccupation, without looking around,

waved his cane behind him warningly to all nature, and said, " Shu!"

The men were now within a few feet of each other. A hen ran across the road before one of them. A feathery seed-vessel, wafted from a wayside tree, fell at the feet of the other. And, unheeding this irony of Nature, the two opponents came nearer, erect and rigid, looked in each other's eyes, and—passed!

Colonel Starbottle had to be lifted from the cart. " This yer camp is played out," he said, gloomily, as he affected to be supported into the " Magnolia ". With what further expression he might have indicated his feelings it was impossible to say, for at that moment Scott joined the group. " Did you speak to me?" he asked of the Colonel, dropping his hand, as if with accidental familiarity, on that gentleman's shoulder. The Colonel, recognizing some occult quality in the touch, and some unknown quantity in the glance of his questioner, contented himself by replying, " No, sir," with dignity. A few rods away, York's conduct was as characteristic and peculiar. " You had a mighty fine chance; why didn't you plump him?" said Jack Hamlin, as York drew near the buggy. " Because I hate him," was the reply, heard only by Jack. Contrary to popular belief, this reply was not hissed between the lips of the speaker, but was said in an ordinary tone. But Jack Hamlin, who was an observer of mankind, noticed that the speaker's hands were cold, and his lips dry, as he helped him into the buggy, and accepted the seeming paradox with a smile.

When Sandy Bar became convinced that the quarrel between York and Scott could not be settled after the usual local methods, it gave no further concern thereto. But presently it was rumoured that the " Amity Claim " was in litigation, and that its possession would be expensively disputed by each of the partners. As it was well known that the claim in question was " worked out " and worthless, and that the partners, whom it had already enriched, had talked of abandoning it but a day or two before the quarrel, this proceeding could only be accounted for as gratuitous spite. Later, two San Francisco lawyers made their appearance in this guileless Arcadia, and were eventually taken into the saloons, and—what was pretty much the same thing—the confidences of the inhabitants. The results of this unhallowed intimacy were many subpœnas; and, indeed, when the " Amity Claim " came to trial, all of Sandy Bar that was not in compulsory attendance at the county seat came there from curiosity. The gulches and ditches for miles around were deserted. I do not propose to describe that already famous trial. Enough that, in the language of the plaintiff's counsel, " it was one of no ordinary significance, involving the inherent rights of that untiring industry which had developed the Pactolian resources of this golden land;" and, in the homelier phrase of Colonel Starbottle, " A fuss that gentlemen might hev settled in ten minutes over a social glass, ef they meant business; or in ten seconds with a revolver, ef they meant fun." Scott got a verdict, from which York instantly appealed. It was said that he had sworn to spend his last dollar in the struggle.

In this way Sandy Bar began to accept the enmity of the former partners as a lifelong feud, and the fact that they had ever been friends was forgotten. The few who expected to learn from the trial the origin of the quarrel were disappointed. Among the various conjectures, that which ascribed some occult feminine influence as the cause was naturally popular, in a camp given to dubious compliment of the sex. " My word for it, gentlemen," said Colonel Starbottle, who had been known in Sacramento as a Gentleman of the Old School, " there's some lovely creature at the bottom of this." The gallant Colonel then proceeded to illustrate his theory, by divers sprightly stories, such as Gentlemen of the Old School are in the habit of repeating, but which, from deference to the prejudices of gentlemen of a more recent school, I refrain from transcribing here. But it would appear that even the Colonel's theory was fallacious. The only woman who personally might have exercised any influence over the partners, was the pretty daughter of " old man Folinsbee ", of Poverty Flat, at whose hospitable house —which exhibited some comforts and refinements rare in that crude civilization—both York and Scott were frequent visitors. Yet into this charming retreat York strode one evening, a month after the quarrel, and, beholding Scott sitting there, turned to the fair hostess with the abrupt query, " Do you love this man?" The young woman thus addressed returned that answer—at once spirited and evasive—which would occur to most of my fair readers in such an exigency. Without another word, York left the house. " Miss Jo " heaved the least possible sigh as the door closed on York's curls and square shoulders, and then, like a good girl, turned to her insulted guest. " But would you believe it, dear?" she afterwards related to an intimate friend, " the other creature, after glowering at me for a moment, got upon its hind legs, took its hat, and left, too; and that's the last I've seen of either."

The same hard disregard of all other interests or feelings in the gratification of their blind rancour characterized all their actions. When York purchased the land below Scott's new claim, and obliged the latter, at a great expense, to make a long detour to carry a " tail-race " around it, Scott retaliated by building a dam that overflowed York's claim on the river. It was Scott, who, in conjunction with Colonel Starbottle, first organized that active opposition to the Chinamen, which resulted in the driving off of York's Mongolian labourers; it was York who built the wagon-road and established the express which rendered Scott's mules and pack-trains obsolete; it was Scott who called into life the Vigilance Committee which expatriated York's friend, Jack Hamlin; it was York who created the *Sandy Bar Herald*, which characterized the act as " a lawless outrage " and Scott as a " Border Ruffian "; it was Scott, at the head of twenty masked men, who, one moonlight night, threw the offending " forms " into the yellow river, and scattered the types in the dusty road. These proceedings were received in the distant and more civilized outlying towns as vague indications of progress and vitality. I have before me a copy of the *Poverty Flat Pioneer* for the week ending August 12, 1856, in which the editor, under the head of " County Improvements ", says: " The new Presbyterian Church on C Street, at Sandy Bar, is completed. It stands upon the lot formerly occupied by the Magnolia Saloon, which was so mysteriously burnt last month. The temple, which now rises like a Phœnix from the ashes of the Magnolia, is virtually the free gift of H. J. York, Esq., of Sandy Bar, who purchased the lot and donated the lumber. Other buildings are going up in the vicinity, but the most noticeable is the ' Sunny South

THE ILIAD OF SANDY BAR 205

Saloon ', erected by Captain Mat. Scott, nearly opposite the church. Captain Scott has spared no expense in the furnishing of this saloon, which promises to be one of the most agreeable places of resort in old Tuolumne. He has recently imported two new, first-class billiard-tables, with cork cushions. Our old friend, ' Mountain Jimmy ', will dispense liquors at the bar. We refer our readers to the advertisement in another column. Visitors to Sandy Bar cannot do better than give ' Jimmy ' a call." Among the local items occurred the following: " H. J. York, Esq., of Sandy Bar, has offered a reward of $100 for the detection of the parties who hauled away the steps of the new Presbyterian Church, C Street, Sandy Bar, during divine service on Sabbath evening last. Captain Scott adds another hundred for the capture of the miscreants who broke the magnificent plate-glass windows of the new saloon on the following evening. There is some talk of reorganizing the old Vigilance Committee at Sandy Bar."

When, for many months of cloudless weather, the hard, unwinking sun of Sandy Bar had regularly gone down on the unpacified wrath of these men, there was some talk of mediation. In particular, the pastor of the church to which I have just referred—a sincere, fearless, but perhaps not fully-enlightened man—seized gladly upon the occasion of York's liberality to attempt to reunite the former partners. He preached an earnest sermon on the abstract sinfulness of discord and rancour. But the excellent sermons of the Rev. Mr. Daws were directed to an ideal congregation that did not exist at Sandy Bar—a congregation of beings of unmixed vices and virtues, of single impulses, and perfectly logical motives, of preternatural simplicity, of childlike faith, and grown-up

responsibilities.   As, unfortunately, the people who
actually attended Mr. Daws's church were mainly very
human, somewhat artful, more self-excusing than self-
accusing, rather good-natured, and decidedly weak, they
quietly shed that portion of the sermon which referred
to themselves, and accepting York and Scott—who were
both in defiant attendance—as curious examples of those
ideal beings above referred to, felt a certain satisfaction
—which, I fear, was not altogether Christian-like—in
their " raking-down ". If Mr. Daws expected York and
Scott to shake hands after the sermon, he was disappointed.
But he did not relax his purpose. With that quiet fear-
lessness and determination which had won for him the
respect of men who were too apt to regard piety as synony-
mous with effeminacy, he attacked Scott in his own house.
What he said has not been recorded, but it is to be feared
that it was part of his sermon. When he had concluded,
Scott looked at him, not unkindly, over the glasses of his
bar, and said, less irreverently than the words might
convey, " Young man, I rather like your style; but when
you know York and me as well as you do God Almighty,
it'll be time to talk."

And so the feud progressed; and so, as in more illustrious examples, the private and personal enmity of two
representative men led gradually to the evolution of some
crude, half-expressed principle or belief. It was not long
before it was made evident that those beliefs were identical
with certain principles laid down by the founders of the
American Constitution, as expounded by the statesman-
like A., or were the fatal quicksands, on which the ship
of state might be wrecked, warningly pointed out by the
eloquent B. The practical result of all which was the

nomination of York and Scott to represent the opposite factions of Sandy Bar in legislative councils.

For some weeks past, the voters of Sandy Bar and the adjacent camps had been called upon, in large type, to " RALLY!" In vain the great pines at the cross-roads—whose trunks were compelled to bear this and other legends—moaned and protested from their windy watch-towers. But one day, with fife and drum, and flaming transparency, a procession filed into the triangular grove at the head of the gulch. The meeting was called to order by Colonel Starbottle, who, having once enjoyed legislative functions, and being vaguely known as a " war-horse ", was considered to be a valuable partisan of York. He concluded an appeal for his friend, with an enunciation of principles, interspersed with one or two anecdotes so gratuitously coarse that the very pines might have been moved to pelt him with their cast-off cones, as he stood there. But he created a laugh, on which his candidate rode into popular notice; and when York rose to speak, he was greeted with cheers. But, to the general astonishment, the new speaker at once launched into bitter denunciation of his rival. He not only dwelt upon Scott's deeds and example, as known to Sandy Bar, but spoke of facts connected with his previous career, hitherto unknown to his auditors. To great precision of epithet and directness of statement, the speaker added the fascination of revelation and exposure. The crowd cheered, yelled, and were delighted, but when this astounding philippic was concluded, there was a unanimous call for " Scott!" Colonel Starbottle would have resisted this manifest impropriety, but in vain. Partly from a crude sense of justice, partly from a meaner craving for excitement, the assemblage was inflexible; and Scott was dragged, pushed, and pulled upon the platform.

As his frowsy head and unkempt beard appeared above the railing, it was evident that he was drunk. But it was also evident, before he opened his lips, that the orator of Sandy Bar—the one man who could touch their vagabond sympathies (perhaps because he was not above appealing to them)—stood before them. A consciousness of this power lent a certain dignity to his figure, and I am not sure but that his very physical condition impressed them as a kind of regal unbending and large condescension. Howbeit, when this unexpected Hector arose from this ditch, York's myrmidons trembled.

" There's naught, gentlemen," said Scott, leaning forward on the railing,—" there's naught as that man hez said as isn't true. I was run outer Cairo; I did belong to the Regulators; I did desert from the army; I did leave a wife in Kansas. But thar's one thing he didn't charge me with, and, maybe, he's forgotten. For three years, gentlemen, I was that man's pardner!—" Whether he intended to say more, I cannot tell; a burst of applause artistically rounded and enforced the climax, and virtually elected the speaker. That Fall he went to Sacramento; York went abroad, and for the first time in many years, distance and a new atmosphere isolated the old antagonists.

With little of change in the green wood, grey rock, and yellow river, but with much shifting of human landmarks, and new faces in its habitations, three years passed over Sandy Bar. The two men, once so identified with its character, seemed to have been quite forgotten. " You will never return to Sandy Bar," said Miss Folinsbee,

the " Lily of Poverty Flat ", on meeting York in Paris,
" for Sandy Bar is no more. They call it Riverside now;
and the new town is built higher up on the river-bank.
By the by, ' Jo ' says that Scott has won his suit about
the ' Amity Claim ', and that he lives in the old cabin,
and is drunk half his time. O, I beg your pardon," added
the lively lady, as a flush crossed York's sallow cheek;
" but, bless me, I really thought that old grudge was
made up. I'm sure it ought to be."

It was three months after this conversation, and a
pleasant summer evening, that the Poverty Flat coach
drew up before the veranda of the Union Hotel at Sandy
Bar. Among its passengers was one, apparently a stranger,
in the local distinction of well-fitting clothes and closely
shaven face, who demanded a private room and retired
early to rest. But before sunrise next morning he arose,
and, drawing some clothes from his carpet-bag, proceeded to array himself in a pair of white duck trousers,
a white duck overshirt, and straw hat. When this toilet
was completed, he tied a red bandanna handkerchief in
a loop and threw it loosely over his shoulders. The
transformation was complete. As he crept softly down
the stairs and stepped into the road, no one would have
detected in him the elegant stranger of the previous
night, and but few have recognized the face and figure of
Henry York of Sandy Bar.

In the uncertain light of that early hour, and in the
change that had come over the settlement, he had to
pause for a moment to recall where he stood. The Sandy
Bar of his recollection lay below him, nearer the river; the
buildings around him were of later date and newer fashion.
As he strode toward the river, he noticed here a schoolhouse
and there a church. A little farther on, " The Sunny

South " came in view, transformed into a restaurant, its gilding faded and its paint rubbed off. He now knew where he was; and running briskly down a declivity, crossed a ditch, and stood upon the lower boundary of the Amity Claim.

The grey mist was rising slowly from the river, clinging to the tree-tops and drifting up the mountain-side, until it was caught among these rocky altars, and held a sacrifice to the ascending sun. At his feet the earth, cruelly gashed and scarred by his forgotten engines, had, since the old days, put on a show of greenness here and there, and now smiled forgivingly up at him, as if things were not so bad after all. A few birds were bathing in the ditch with a pleasant suggestion of its being a new and special provision of Nature, and a hare ran into an inverted sluice-box, as he approached, as if it were put there for that purpose.

He had not yet dared to look in a certain direction. But the sun was now high enough to paint the little eminence on which the cabin stood. In spite of his self-control, his heart beat faster as he raised his eyes toward it. Its window and door were closed, no smoke came from its *adobe* chimney, but it was else unchanged. When within a few yards of it, he picked up a broken shovel, and shouldering it with a smile, strode toward the door and knocked. There was no sound from within. The smile died upon his lips as he nervously pushed the door open.

A figure started up angrily and came toward him,— a figure whose bloodshot eyes suddenly fixed into a vacant stare, whose arms were at first outstretched and then thrown up in warning gesticulation,—a figure that suddenly gasped, choked, and then fell forward in a fit.

But before he touched the ground, York had him out into the open air and sunshine. In the struggle, both fell and rolled over on the ground. But the next moment York was sitting up, holding the convulsed frame of his former partner on his knee, and wiping the foam from his inarticulate lips. Gradually the tremor became less frequent, and then ceased; and the strong man lay unconscious in his arms.

For some moments York held him quietly thus, looking in his face. Afar, the stroke of a woodman's axe—a mere phantom of sound—was all that broke the stillness. High up the mountain, a wheeling hawk hung breathlessly above them. And then came voices, and two men joined them.

"A fight?" No, a fit; and would they help him bring the sick man to the hotel?

And there, for a week, the stricken partner lay, unconscious of aught but the visions wrought by disease and fear. On the eighth day, at sunrise, he rallied, and, opening his eyes, looked upon York, and pressed his hand; then he spoke:

"And it's you. I thought it was only whisky."

York replied by taking both of his hands, boyishly working them backward and forward, as his elbow rested on the bed, with a pleasant smile.

"And you've been abroad. How did you like Paris?"

"So, so. How did *you* like Sacramento?"

"Bully!"

And that was all they could think to say. Presently Scott opened his eyes again.

"I'm mighty weak."

"You'll get better soon."

"Not much."

A long silence followed, in which they could hear the sounds of wood-chopping, and that Sandy Bar was already astir for the coming day. Then Scott slowly and with difficulty turned his face to York, and said,—

" I might hev killed you once."

" I wish you had."

They pressed each other's hands again, but Scott's grasp was evidently failing. He seemed to summon his energies for a special effort.

" Old man!"

" Old chap."

" Closer!"

York bent his head toward the slowly-fading face.

" Do ye mind that morning?"

" Yes."

A gleam of fun slid into the corner of Scott's blue eye, as he whispered,—

" Old man, thar *was* too much saleratus in that bread."

It is said that these were his last words. For when the sun, which had so often gone down upon the idle wrath of these foolish men, looked again upon them reunited, it saw the hand of Scott fall cold and irresponsive from the yearning clasp of his former partner, and it knew that the feud of Sandy Bar was at an end.